SHADOW OF A DOUBT

Fiction Titles from Jane McLoughlin

COINCIDENCE
A TURN IN THE ROAD
THE FURIES
THE HIDE AND SEEK CORPSE
DEATH BY PREJUDICE
STRANGER IN THE HOUSE
CHEATED HEARTS
THE UNFORGIVEN

SHADOW OF
A DOUBT

Jane McLoughlin

This first world edition published 2010
in Great Britain and in the USA by
SEVERN HOUSE PUBLISHERS LTD of
9–15 High Street, Sutton, Surrey, England, SM1 1DF.

British Library Cataloguing in Publication Data

McLoughlin, Jane.
  Shadow of a doubt.
  1. Police – England – Devon – Fiction. 2. Murder –
  Investigation – Fiction. 3. DNA fingerprinting – Fiction.
  4. Detective and mystery stories.
  I. Title
  823.9'14-dc22

ISBN-13: 978-0-7278-6951-7   (cased)

All Severn House titles are printed on acid-free paper.

Severn House Publishers support The Forest Stewardship Council [FSC],
the leading international forest certification organisation. All our titles that
are printed on Greenpeace-approved FSC-certified paper carry the FSC logo.

Mixed Sources
Product group from well-managed
forests and other controlled sources
www.fsc.org Cert no. SA-COC-1565
© 1996 Forest Stewardship Council

FSC

Typeset by Palimpsest Book Production Ltd.,
Falkirk, Stirlingshire.
Printed and bound in Great Britain by the
MPG Books Group, Bodmin, Cornwall.

To my friend Sally Vincent,
who has shown me what the word means.

ONE

March 2004

Everyone in the group looked similar in the cold light of very early morning; grey men and women all with woolly hats pulled down over their ears, big clumsy gloves, and anorak collars turned up around pinched faces washed-out in the pitiless pale glare of dawn.

People stamped their feet, trying to get the circulation going in freezing toes; they puffed out their cheeks and released their breath like a group of horses waiting to go into battle. They had nothing to say.

And then the great brash orange sun drifted above the black silhouette of fir trees across the top of the hill, looking so like a climbing hot air balloon that, when one of the men in the group said, 'I wish it was and I was in it,' everyone knew what he meant. Some laughed and it helped to relieve the tension.

A police Land-Rover appeared from the common, bucking down the rutted track like a lifeboat in a rough sea. As it stopped and a police inspector jumped out, the waiting group were suddenly transformed. They began to mutter amongst themselves, pressing forward to hear how they were to go about what they were there to do.

The police inspector was in his late forties and this morning he looked like an old man. His eyes were raw from lack of sleep and his voice sounded thin, like a chronic invalid's. He didn't smile.

'Thank you for turning out to help this morning,' he said. 'As you all know, we're here to search for Julie Makepeace.' His voice faltered, he had young children of his own, then he went on, 'This young girl has been missing now for five days,' he said, 'and it's vital we find her soon. The weather's bad and the forecast's worse, and if she's lying hurt somewhere . . .' The tight, thin voice died away while the inspector swallowed hard and coughed, then went on. 'But apart from that, we're also looking for anything which might give us a clue as to where she is and what's happened to her. Anything she might have dropped, anything she might have been wearing or could belong to her . . .'

'What's he talking about?' a man standing next to Angus Dillon asked. 'Is he trying to say we should pick up used condoms and stuff like that? That's what most people who come on to Studleigh Common at this time of year are here for, isn't it?'

'I don't think a rapist would bother with a condom,' Angus said mildly. He understood that his neighbour's inappropriate facetiousness was a way of dealing with the apprehension they all felt.

But a pale young woman with dark hair in a ponytail standing nearby turned on them. 'Don't talk like that,' she snarled. 'Have a bit of decency, can't you.'

'We're out here looking for her, aren't we?' the man beside Angus said, 'what more do you want? Let's get on with it.'

He moved away, his nicotine-stained moustache bristling.

The young woman said to Angus, 'I'm sorry. I didn't mean . . .'

Tears were streaming down her face in the way women cry when they are in despair and crying becomes a kind of protracted background to their ordinary everyday doings.

Angus didn't dare try to comfort her. He was embarrassed by her emotion. All his life he had been worried when women lost control of their emotions. He felt he was expected to do something, but he didn't know what.

'Come on,' he said, giving her a clumsy pat on the shoulder, 'we're wasting time. We're not going to find her standing here and talking about it.'

The rest of the group were already moving, fanning out across the common through spiky black stems of winter heather and wet bracken, and dark thorny gorse bushes.

'It's not my idea of a place to bring a girl for sex,' Angus said suddenly, and was horrified that he had spoken aloud.

'I'm sorry,' he said, 'it was what that man said, I didn't think.'

She surprised him by smiling. 'It's all right,' she said, 'for some reason it makes me feel better to hear you say something normal like that. I'm Sarah Makepeace, by the way.'

'Makepeace?' Angus said, 'Isn't that the name of . . .?'

'Yes,' Sarah said, 'Julie was my niece.'

Angus didn't know what to say. Then he said, 'Is. *Is*. We're going to find her.'

She nodded and strode off across the common at a slight angle to the rest of the group, who were now strung out across the dead bracken and the heather.

Angus followed her, trying to keep his gaze fixed on the ground in front of his feet in case he missed a vital clue. His spectacles misted up and kept slipping down his nose, making it hard for him to see where he was going.

They went in silence for a while. Then Sarah said, 'It's hard going, isn't it? This sandy soil's very difficult to walk on, and the pebbles on the path make it worse. I keep tripping over rabbit holes and it shifts under my feet.'

'It's bloody hard,' he said, 'but at least it would explain how Julie might've fallen and twisted her ankle or something. Keep going.'

They trudged on. It seemed to Angus that this terrain must be like the surface of the moon, except that on the moon there weren't tracts of gorse and heather with thorns and spikes out to get you. He was wearing Wellington boots and knew already that after today they would never be watertight again. He'd been stupid to wear them in a place like this. It wasn't just the thorns making holes; they were uncomfortable to walk in. His feet were freezing. He'd have been better off in something like Sarah's climbing boots, except he didn't have any. He felt irritable and found himself disliking her because she was part of the reason he was here and he wished he weren't.

But Sarah, too, seemed to be having trouble making her way across the common. At the top of a small rise she stopped and flopped on to the ground. 'My God,' she said, putting up her hands to release the clip on her ponytail and then tie it up again. 'How do people climb real mountains in these things, I've got blisters already?'

Angus sat down beside her and pulled a flask out of his hip pocket. 'Help yourself,' he said, 'it'll dull the pain.'

Sarah took a swig from the flask. She's a drinker, anyway, thank God, Angus thought, there's none of that coy little choking thing women do, pretending the liquor's so strong it takes their breath away.

'That's better,' Sarah said. The whisky had brought a little colour to her face. She handed him back the flask. 'The trouble is,' she said, 'these boots aren't my size. They belong to a friend at work, and her feet are bigger than mine, so they're rubbing.'

Angus took a drink and felt his dislike of her melt away. Their search for a missing child was a grim mission and he was glad she was there keeping him company. Then he told himself, actually, I'm glad I'm here to keep her company, she's the one who needs it. And he thought, that's the first time in ages I've thought of how someone else is feeling without consciously making myself do it.

He felt he had to distract them from their feet.

'I wish I weren't so unfit,' he said. 'I'm afraid I've let myself go. I should take more exercise, but if this is what exercise is like, I'm glad I don't. I spend too much time in front of a computer, or in the pub.' He lit a cigarette and added, 'Where do you work? Are you from the village?'

'Born and bred,' she said. 'But I go to Hunsteignton three days a week to work in an architect's office. It's in the town centre, near the war memorial.'

'I don't go about much,' Angus said. 'The street market used to be fun.'

He took another long draught from the flask. He saw her look startled at how much he seemed to need it.

'Medicinal,' he said, 'whisky's good for you, all that basic barley.' He smiled and she smiled back.

'I thought barley was fattening,' she said. 'You're incredibly thin, aren't you?'

'Am I?' he said, surprised. 'I hadn't noticed.'

She laughed. 'I think you've just put your finger on one of the fundamental differences between men and women,' she said.

'There's a bit more to it than that, I'm afraid,' he said, thinking that if he hadn't noticed how much weight he'd lost over the last few months, his wife hadn't seemed aware of it either. Well, enough of that.

He said to Sarah, 'So you're an architect? I always wanted to be an architect when I was a kid.'

'So did I, but I'm not, I'm just a hanger-on, I work in the office. What about you?'

'Oh,' he said, 'this and that. We live in Otterbrook, out on the Hunsteignton road. My wife Joan commutes to town every day. She's a solicitor. She's got a case in court today, that's why she isn't here.'

Angus was trying to divert any more questions about himself. He didn't want to have to explain what he had not yet fully taken in and rationalized about himself, that the week before he had been sacked from his job on the local weekly paper for his drinking. He couldn't take this seriously. All journalists drank too much, it was part of the job. And yet he had been fired. He still kidded himself it was some sort of joke, that the editor would call him one day soon and ask him why he hadn't turned up at his desk that morning, there was work to be done.

He offered the flask to Sarah, but she shook her head, getting stiffly to her feet. 'Better not,' she said, 'we'd best get moving.'

He started to scramble upright and she offered him her hand to help him up. They were both suddenly horribly conscious of why they were there.

'Yes,' he said, 'let's go.'

The sun had now risen high above the dark line of fir trees on the top of the hill. In the valley where Angus could see the rest of the search party fanned out across the scrub of heather and gorse, a thin bank of mist hovering a foot or so above the ground made it look to him as though they were wading through waves breaking on a dark-pebbled shore.

'That poor child,' he said suddenly, 'how awful not to see how beautiful nature is.'

He was startled again, as soon as he heard himself say this, that he had spoken aloud.

He stammered something, trying to take back the awful finality of what he'd said.

Sarah put up her hand to stop him saying anything more.

'It's all right,' she said. 'You do think she's dead, don't you?'

'Yes,' he said.

'I do too,' she said. 'I pretend I don't when I'm with my sister-in-law, Julie's mother, but I can't help it. I just can't make myself believe she could be alive now.'

They tramped on for a while in silence through a copse of silver birch trees, whose slim, elegant, white trunks looked to Angus like a chorus in a Greek tragedy waiting to take up some lament about disaster.

'I didn't mean . . .' he said.

'I'd rather you said what you think,' she said. 'People keep forcing us to look on the bright side, keep up our hopes, saying Julie's just run off and she'll come home as soon as she's ready, and I feel I'm somehow betraying her if I don't go along with it. I feel that if I even admit I think she could be dead, she will be. I'm glad you said what you really think. Somehow it makes me feel I can allow myself to face the truth, whatever it is.'

Angus offered her a cigarette.

'I don't smoke,' she said. 'Not even now.'

He lit one for himself, drawing the smoke deep into his lungs with a sense of relief.

For some time they walked on without speaking. The track they were following wound round the edge of the common, so they were gradually working their way towards a meeting with the main search party which had come over the top of the hill. The sandy terrain was honeycombed with rabbit burrows amongst the gorse and heather, but on the open ground there were few places where anyone could be hidden.

'What are we doing here?' Sarah said at last. She sounded close to tears. 'A helicopter would do a much better job in quarter the time. After all, what kind of clues are we looking for?'

Angus took out his flask again and they both drank from it. He kicked the soil and sand sprayed from his boot. 'It's the sort of place where it would be quite easy to bury a body,' he said, glaring accusingly at the ground.

Sarah looked terrified at the way he said this. She bit her lip. 'I suppose you're right,' she said quietly.

Angus handed her the stub of the cigarette he was smoking. 'Take a puff,' he said, 'it'll calm you down.'

She shook her head, but she did take it and try to inhale. She spluttered and handed it back. 'It's an acquired skill, smoking,' she said. 'I don't know how.'

'Let's try to be logical,' he said. 'Suppose you were burying . . . something . . . and you didn't want to be seen, you'd make for cover, wouldn't you?'

'The fir trees?'

'Well, yes, maybe, but it's hard digging under fir trees, the soil's all roots.' Angus wondered where this sudden arboricultural expertise of his came from. He said, 'You'd be looking for light sandy soil and cover as well.'

They both stood and stared at the near distance for such a place. 'Under silver birches,' Angus said.

He pointed back the way they had come. The slim white chorus of trees swayed as though narrating tragedy.

'But we've already been there?'

Angus wanted to forget what he had just said and move on, away from his own sudden certainty that they had missed something vital. He wanted to go on. No one would ever know that he had denied the pitiless intimation of disaster that possessed him now. No one could blame him. Sarah herself had said it: 'We've already been there.'

But he shook his head. 'We've got to go back,' he said, 'we weren't looking properly, we just went through the motions. We didn't go off the track.'

He started to run back to the silver birch trees, leaping clumsily across the scrub. He didn't know if she would follow him, but then he heard her heavy breathing behind him as she tried to keep up.

He was the one who found the child's body. She was buried behind a fallen, half-rotted silver birch. Someone had dug a shallow grave and then, as the dry sandy soil fell back into the pit, had laid the child's body in it and tried to cover it. But the foxes had found it and exposed Julie's leg, bare except for a blue sock and pink trainer.

Angus retched, then turned away and caught Sarah's arm as she came up to him.

'No,' he said. 'Don't look, please don't look.'

She pulled away from him and stared into his face.

'Is she . . .?'

He nodded.

She started to say the child's name, 'Julie, Julie, Julie,' over and over again.

'You can't do anything,' he said. He took out his flask and held it against her clenched teeth until he forced her to drink. 'You've got to go and get the others,' he said.

'No,' she said, whimpering, 'you go. I'll stay with her. She loved me. Poor little girl.'

'I'll stay with her,' he said. 'You're younger and fitter than me, you'll be quicker. Keep shouting, they'll hear you before you catch up with them.'

For a moment he thought she was going to ignore him and push him aside to see what he was trying to screen with his body, but then she turned and ran out of the trees towards the open common. He heard that she was screaming as she ran.

Soon, though, he began to be aware of oppressive and unnatural silence. Angus was used to the small sounds of normal quiet when he was alone in the country – the rustle of a small animal in undergrowth, the twittering of birds, the creaking of leafless trees in a breath of wind. But now there was nothing; it was as though everything living was holding its breath because of the affront to nature lying behind the rotting trunk of the fallen silver birch.

Angus finished the whisky in his flask; he smoked all the cigarettes he had left, lighting one from the stump of the last, until the pack was empty and he threw it away. As he threw down the last butt, he thought, thank God it's not summer or I could've set light to the whole bloody common. He stamped the cigarette into the ground.

He tried not to look at the poor little shoe and the blue sock he couldn't help seeing sticking out of the sand. He knew that he must not touch the body, much as he wished he could scoop silvery sand over Julie's exposed leg.

He found himself talking aloud to her, trying to lift the unnerving silence.

'What did you do to your knee?' he asked her. 'That must've hurt, a big graze like that.'

Then he said, 'I'm sorry it's only me, Julie, you'd probably have been better off with Sarah, or one of the policemen or someone, but I thought it best to get someone to look after you as soon as possible, and Sarah's quicker than me. I'm so sorry. I wish I didn't smoke and drink and then I might've been more use to you.' And then he said, 'What happened to you, Julie? Who did this to you?' and he heard himself sounding as though he were pleading with the child.

My God, he thought, anyone hearing me going on like this would think I was maudlin drunk. He heard his own voice repeating again and again, 'Oh, please, please, someone come, someone come and help her.'

TWO

May 2009

'I'm going to have to run for my train,' Sean Miller said. 'Don't you have a home to go to?'

He and Joan Dillon, who worked with him, had come into a wine bar close to the Magistrates Court in Hunsteignton for a quick drink to celebrate winning a case that afternoon. But when Sean began to gather his belongings to leave, Joan made no move to go with him.

'I'll hang on here for a while,' she said. 'It's still rush hour, the traffic out of town will be horrendous.'

She watched Sean hurry off, briefcase in hand, to catch the Axminster train which would take him back to his cheery overweight wife and their new baby. In spite of herself, she envied him. Not the wife and the sleepless nights up with the baby, but the domestic contentment he positively exuded. Once, Joan thought, the highlight of my day, too, was going home to Angus, looking forward to spending the evening together, talking about everything and anything, making each other laugh.

'It's a hell of a long time since I felt like that,' she said, and only realized that she had spoken aloud when the young woman sitting beside her at the counter turned and smiled at her.

'Sorry,' the young woman said, 'I didn't hear what you said.'

She looks nice, Joan thought. The girl had a lot of soft wavy dark brown hair and a wide calcium-rich smile; a real healthy country girl who looked willing to be friendly. Joan still felt herself an outsider among the locals, even though she'd been living here for more than twelve years and been married to Angus, the quintessential native son, for ten. For most of those years, she was pleased not to be accepted by these people; indeed she'd taken care to underline that she was different. Hence the power suits and the haircut from *Sex and the City*, and the absurdly high heels she had to buy on the Internet because the shops in the county town didn't stock anything that far removed from country life.

Joan looked at this nice-looking, pretty young woman whose clear eyes and fresh skin appeared never to have breathed city air in her whole life. She had certainly never bought designer gear on the Internet, but she brought a style of her own to her dark Marks and Spencer skirt and plain white shirt. Joan wondered what the girl must make of her: a woman past her prime clinging to youth, someone trying to impose what she wanted to be on what she really was.

'I'm sorry,' Joan said, 'I didn't realize I was thinking aloud.'

She hasn't really even looked at me, Joan told herself, I'm part of the scenery, just someone to pass time with in a bar on the way home to her real life. And she thought, where did it all go? I could have done things differently. I wanted an excuse to be unhappy so Angus would take me back to London, but he couldn't.

The girl with the smile said, 'I do that all the time. I talk to the cat at home, and sometimes I forget where I am when I'm out and find I've said something to him and people are looking at me like I'm crazy.'

Joan laughed. 'I wish I had a cat,' she said, 'but I've got a husband.'

'Surely that's more rewarding than unburdening yourself to the cat? I'm not saying Sock's not a great listener, but he hasn't got much to say for himself.'

The girl smiled, and Joan was suddenly reminded of how good it had been, first when she was a student and then as a newly qualified solicitor, to have girlfriends to talk to. It hadn't really struck her until now how much she missed those no holds barred confessionals with the young women in their shared flats. She'd lost touch with all of them over the years since she left London; they'd moved on themselves, married and given up work to have kids, or taken up high-powered jobs and moved abroad.

And now Joan, sitting with a stranger in a shabby wine bar in a modest provincial town, felt bereft. She'd been left behind, and now she had nothing to show for all those youthful aspirations. She was afraid that she might actually start to weep.

The girl with the smile briefly touched Joan's arm. She had nice eyes, too, grey with a greenish fleck. 'We might as well make the best of it while we can,' she said quietly. 'Neither one of us seems to have anyone at home who's an inspiring conversationalist, so let's have another drink and talk to each other.'

She ordered a bottle of red wine, and then, because the wine bar was filling up and people were pressing forward to the bar counter to get served, they moved to a table in a corner by a window looking over a street crowded with people on their way home. Joan stared at them. She wondered, why do they all look as if they've got somewhere they want to be? And I don't?

She turned away from the window and smiled at the girl. For a while, the two women faced each other across the table in silence, embarrassed that an unguarded moment of intimacy between strangers had led them to expect from each other something that neither could fulfil.

Joan did not know what to say to this young woman, who was about twenty years her junior. She felt old, as though at forty-eight she was on the verge of senility. She thought, why's a girl her age being nice to me?

'I'm Sarah,' the girl said, 'I work in the office at Savill's, the architects in the town centre. I like my job but it's not going to lead to anything. I'm twenty-six, I live in one of those two-up two-down Victorian terraces on the Deepditch Road, I've got a cat called Sock and, at the moment, that's about it. And yes, I know it sounds boring, sometimes I bore myself thinking about my life. How sad is that? Now it's your turn.'

'Do you have someone?' Joan asked her. 'A boyfriend?'

'I suppose so,' Sarah said, 'but he's just that, a friend who happens to be a lover. He's called Jeff and he's a reporter on the *Clarion*. He's at home when I'm at work and when I'm home he's working, and that includes most weekends.'

'Another journalist?' Joan said. 'Something we've got in common, anyway. My husband was a reporter. Does Jeff feel the same way as you, about being friends rather than lovers?'

Joan thought to herself how odd it was to be asking these personal questions of a stranger who wasn't a client.

Sarah hesitated, then smiled. 'No,' she said, 'he's ambitious. He can't wait to move on and get a job in London and change the world. Oh, I think he thinks I'll go with him and be his unpaid housekeeper for life, but that's not for me. Not with him, anyway.'

Joan laughed. 'God, I remember feeling like that. If only I'd taken more notice. I'm Joan, by the way, Joan Dillon. I'm a partner at Digby and Pratt, the solicitors round the corner from the courthouse, and I'm just about old enough to be your mother, except when I was the right age for that to be true I was studying far too hard to think of boys. I'm married to a man called Angus. And I'm fed up with everything.'

'Everything?'

Joan wasn't sure from Sarah's tone if the young woman was laughing at her.

'No, you're right,' Joan said, 'it's not everything that's wrong, it's just me. Someone else might be quite happy with what I've got, it's my fault I'm not. Only, I feel there should be some way I could do something to make things better, but I don't know what it is.'

'Me, too,' Sarah said. She filled both their glasses from the bottle of wine and went on, 'If I believed what I read in women's magazines, we're both suffering from low self-esteem and it's up to us to pull ourselves together and do something about it. But I don't really want to do anything about it.'

Joan grinned. 'What, take up hang-gliding or get involved in politics or find a new man, that kind of thing?'

'I've never managed to stay awake long enough to find out what they have in mind, but I suppose so,' Sarah said, laughing.

Joan smiled. Her habitual discontented expression was transformed by the sudden smile, which crossed her face as swiftly as a shaft of sunlight and then disappeared under another cloud. 'Trouble is with that kind of advice,' she said, 'everything they suggest is just papering over the cracks in our lives. As well as offering convenient excuses for killing ourselves. I don't need telling that what's wrong with my life is that I don't like being me. But I don't seem to be able to do much about it. I can't just blame Angus.'

Looking at Sarah's face when she said Angus's name, Joan realized too late that something about the way she spoke had told the girl too much. She began to babble, trying to repair the damage.

'It's not Angus's fault. We don't really talk any more,' Joan said. 'We just don't see each other all that much these days. He spends his evenings out trying to make contacts and pick up stories that might make a paragraph somewhere, and I have to leave for work before he gets up in the mornings.'

Sarah smiled. 'How long have you been married?' she asked.

'Ten years. We met in London seventeen years ago, and moved in together. He was doing shifts on various national newspapers then, hoping someone would give him a job, but it didn't work out. So we moved down here. He came from here originally. He got himself a job on the local paper. We got married and bought a house on the outskirts of Otterbrook, and I started working for Digby and Pratt and here we are.'

'What happened?' Sarah asked.

Joan was tempted to tell her to mind her own business, but in spite of herself she found herself trying to answer the question.

'Nothing. That's the trouble. It was hard for Angus, after London and everything he'd hoped to do,' she said. 'You know, coming back here to write up weddings and funerals. He tried, but he couldn't really take it seriously. I think it happens to journalists and people like that who kind of live their work, you know what I mean? Their work is who they are. If they're not doing well, they get depressed and have some sort of identity crisis. At least they do if they can't see a way of getting back their lives. Angus drank a bit, you know, to blur the edges. Quite a bit in fact, although he was never really drunk, well, hardly ever, anyway, just sort of blunted, but they fired him.'

Sarah nodded. 'And then?' she prompted Joan.

Joan stared at her drink. 'It wasn't money,' she said. 'I earned enough. I suppose it was some sort of male pride thing, you know, the usual psychobabble, being dependent emasculated him. He couldn't forgive me then and he never has. He thinks he's a failure and he's angry, and it's easy to take it out on me. He claims he's writing a book but if I ask how it's going he snaps my head off, and I don't think he is writing anything, really. But he gave up drink and he grubs around for what freelancing he can get, but we couldn't get by without my money and I think he hates me for that. Everything I say he takes the wrong way. Most of the time we scarcely speak.'

'That's sad,' Sarah said. 'Sad for you both.'

'I didn't try to stop him drinking,' Joan said, carried away by her need to express her feelings and now apparently hardly aware of Sarah. 'Drinking was part of what I loved about him, we had a lot of fun. Oh, he was larger than life, the life and soul of the party everywhere we went.'

Her face was transformed by the memory of those heady days, but then it seemed to shut down again on that glimpse of former happiness. She said in a flat voice, 'But something happened – something apart from losing his job – and he stopped drinking and he's a completely different person. We're like strangers now.'

'What was it that happened?' Sarah asked.

She spoke so quietly that Joan could scarcely hear her.

Joan thought for a moment, then said, 'Oh, it must've been building up for ages, but then there was one incident which sort of brought it to a head. A child went missing, a little girl. You may remember? A few years ago. Angus and a lot of local people volunteered to search and Angus found her. It was ages ago, but still it's almost as though he feels that by finding her body he'd made himself responsible for her death.'

Sarah had gone white with shock. She stared at Joan, remembering a bleak stretch of the common on a cold grey early morning, a copse of silver birch trees trembling in the wind, and a man who had shared his flask of whisky with her, and tried to calm her by making her smoke a cigarette as he screened Julie's body from her.

Joan noticed Sarah's silence and looked up at her.

'What's wrong?' she said. 'I'm sorry, did I say something to upset you?'

Sarah shook her head. 'The little girl was called Julie, and she was my niece,' she said. She swallowed the rest of her drink quickly. 'Sorry, what you said suddenly brought it all back, that's all. It's so weird, out of the blue like that. I'd almost forgotten, except of course you never do. Forget, I mean. I've tried to blank it out ever since. I was on that search party. I was with your husband when he found her.'

'My God,' Joan said, 'I'm so sorry. I'd never have mentioned it if I'd known . . .'

'Oh, no, it's all right,' Sarah assured her, 'it was because of him I've been able to get over it. He was kind to me, I was grateful. He sent me away to get help. I wanted to stay but he made me go. He gave me a drink and a cigarette, but I couldn't smoke it. It's the only time I've tried smoking.'

'He still smokes,' Joan said, and smiled. 'That was the trouble, in a way. At least it made it much worse. The police found a cigarette butt near Julie's body and when they found Angus's DNA on it, they thought he must be the murderer. They'd done DNA tests on all the men in the village to eliminate them when the poor child first went missing, and Angus's matched the cigarette butt. It was probably natural enough that they suspected him.'

Sarah said, 'Anyone would have smoked, left there to wait with Julie's body. Any smoker, anyway. That didn't make him a murderer. How could they even think that?'

'The police accepted that in the end, they didn't press charges. But all that didn't help. They kept taking him in for questioning, and people talk. And then the cops didn't

find who did it, so . . . People always want to believe the
worst, don't they, even when there's obviously an innocent
explanation?'

'That's ridiculous,' Sarah said. She sounded angry. 'Why
didn't they ask me? I could've told them he was smoking
when he found her.'

'I don't suppose he even mentioned you'd been there.
He probably thought you'd been through enough already.
He's never mentioned to me that there was someone with
him at the time.'

'The bloody cops knew where I was. They could've
asked,' Sarah said.

'Everyone was upset, even the police,' Joan said. 'I mean,
she was a child. People aren't rational about someone killing
a child. Everyone wanted someone to blame. It blew over.
At least, everything seemed to go back to normal, but Angus
hasn't been the same since. Perhaps if they'd ever found
out who did it he could've moved on, but they didn't, and
he can't.'

Sarah remembered the rather seedy-looking man who had
tried to protect her that terrible day. A very thin man whose
hair needed cutting, wearing spectacles which made his
eyes look like a fish. She would never have placed him as
this neat, carefully made up woman's husband. She remembered she'd felt sorry for him. He'd been wearing gumboots
and his feet were obviously freezing, and he looked almost
blue with cold. He so obviously hadn't wanted to be there
but he was determined to do what he could to help.

'That's horrible,' Sarah said. 'How could anyone imagine
. . . He was a lovely man, the last person on earth who
could've murdered anyone, I'd say.'

She was disconcerted to see Joan's eyes fill with tears. The
older woman could not hide her bitterness as she burst out:
'He was, I know he was, but he isn't that lovely man any
more. My Angus is as dead as that poor child and I miss him.
I'd do anything to have him back, but it's too late. Whoever
killed your poor little niece murdered my husband too.'

THREE

Angus saw the lights of Joan's car as she turned in through the gate. There was five minutes still to go before the end of the programme he was watching on TV, and for a moment he was tempted to stay and see the end.

But it was no good. He got up and turned off the television before retreating upstairs to his study. He couldn't face seeing her. At least they would bicker about things that did not matter to either of them; at best they would make polite embarrassed conversation, like two people forced to share a sleeper on a train.

If he was in his study, she would take it for granted that he was working on his book and leave him alone.

He thought, I wonder if she really believes I'm writing a book? Probably not, he told himself. Joan was as keen as he was to avoid the bitter silent confrontation that was spending an evening together.

Poor Joan, he thought, I was the one who made her like this. I should never have married her, or brought her here. She used to tell me she'd never be able to fit in. She always went on about how she wasn't like other people here, women who kept dogs and liked gardening and drank coffee for charity. She didn't know what to say to them and they didn't understand her. All the women talked about was their husbands, or their houses, or their children, and she'd never been interested in getting married, or in children, and she couldn't wait to get out of the house every day to go to work. She's never really been interested in me, either, he told himself, I was the one who wanted to be married.

Angus remembered how he'd laughed at her, teasing her that she should be in her element, being able to bad-mouth him as a husband to those other women. From what he'd heard, they never had a good word to say about their own men. Joan had gone silent on him then. She'd tried to explain how he didn't understand, she couldn't pretend to be someone she wasn't, and it would be utter failure for her if she had to smother her own independent identity and settle for being seen as a wife. All those other women seemed to accept that they had merged with their husbands and children. They were content with that, and Joan wasn't; Joan was a discrete whole, and so should Angus be. For her, marriage didn't change that.

Too late, he tried to make her tell him what marriage did mean to her. Usually she prevaricated. Then once, exasperated, she told him: 'Nothing. It never meant anything to me. I thought it meant something to you, that's why I did it.'

Angus was surprised that she used her married name at work, until she told him that the partners at Digby and Pratt did not promote single women employees, they were 'unstable'. He'd tried to tell her she didn't have to play his wife, that she had her own identity through her work, and then, to his horror, she'd started to cry and lashed out, mumbling something about how a piddling little provincial solicitor's job wasn't the kind of persona she'd had in mind for herself, and he'd let her down because she'd fallen in love with a journalist who promised he was going to change the world and he'd turned into a small-town hack who'd given up on both their dreams.

And then he'd shouted at her to go and find herself a lover, if that was what this was about, and she'd started screaming that he'd trapped her in a place where there wasn't even anyone she could have a fling with, and don't think she hadn't tried.

That was five years ago at least, and it was the last time a real relationship, flawed as it was, had existed between them. Since then they skirted round each other, like two different species sharing a waterhole.

Angus turned on his computer, pretending to himself that he might try to work; except he had nothing to write.

She wasn't mistaken about me, he thought, I did give up on my dreams. I'm a failure and I always was. But if Joan hadn't kept telling me I was, I might've tried to prove to myself I wasn't. She took all my confidence away. And then he thought, I'm quite happy being a failure; for me, win or lose, it's *not* taking part that counts.

He heard Joan come upstairs, although he could tell she'd taken off those silly high heels of hers so he wouldn't hear her. Then she went into the bathroom. He looked at his watch. She was later than usual tonight. He wondered if something had happened at work to hold her up, or perhaps the traffic had been bad. He typed his own name into Google to pass the time, listening for her to go downstairs again. He had some distinguished namesakes – a man who filmed ocelots in Belize, an Australian political activist – and he was comforted by the association.

How long was Joan going to take? Inevitably, because she was in the bathroom, he wanted to use it.

He typed in Joan's name. Even in Google, she trumped him. A high-flyer in the champagne trade, and a woman who ran her own law firm in the United States. A stranger called Joan Dillon who could conceivably have been his own Joan if she had never lumbered herself with him.

It was no good, he had to go. He got up and went to the door of his study, opening it a little to listen. He could hear nothing.

He hurried across the landing to the bathroom. Joan came out as he was about to knock on the door.

'Hallo,' she said. 'I thought you must be working.'

'I am,' he said. 'I wasn't sure if you'd come in or not. There's cold beef in the fridge, or have you eaten?'

'Thanks, yes. I'm glad I've seen you, actually. I wanted to tell you, I went for a drink after work and met a girl called Sarah who remembers you.'

'I don't remember her,' he said. His first reaction was to find even a girl's memory of him as intrusive.'I don't know anyone called Sarah.'

Joan wouldn't meet his eyes. 'No,' she said, 'you didn't know her, you met her. But she seems to think you helped her and she's wanted to thank you for years. Sarah Makepeace. She was related to that poor child, the one you found . . .'

A distant scene stirred in Angus's memory. Absurd, really, when he'd lived for years with a vivid and total recall of that day on the common, which he was never really able to blank from his mind. A dark-haired girl with a white face and frightened eyes swallowing whisky from his flask and choking on a cigarette; a girl he had treated quite brutally because he wanted her to go away, so he no longer had to protect her from that pathetic ugly fact lying half-hidden under the fallen trunk of a rotting silver birch.

'Oh, yes,' he said, 'I do remember. Poor little thing.'

Joan wasn't sure if he meant the murdered child or Sarah. He wasn't sure himself.

'I liked her,' Joan said.

Angus looked astonished, and Joan guessed why and felt ashamed that this was the first time she had said she liked anyone in all the time they'd lived down here in the Devon wilderness.

'Yes,' Angus said, 'I think I liked her too.'

'I've asked her to dinner on Saturday,' Joan said, preparing to do battle against Angus's expected refusal to be there. He had become almost reclusive since he gave up drinking. 'She's bringing a friend to make the fourth.'

But Angus surprised her. 'That's good,' he said. 'As long as she doesn't want to talk about what happened.'

'She was the child's father's sister,' Joan said. 'It's her tragedy, not yours. It'll be up to her.'

FOUR

'Who are these people?' Neil Carver asked. He was driving too fast on the country road. Once the street lights disappeared as they left Hunsteignton behind, the darkness beyond the beams of the headlamps seemed to promise a collision with a looming wall of vegetation at every bend.

Sarah was wishing she had never agreed to go to dinner with Joan Dillon and her husband. She told herself, it's all very well passing the time of day with a stranger over a bottle of wine in a bar, but an entirely different thing going to someone's home as though we're friends.

And anyway, it wasn't because she wanted to get to know Joan better that Sarah had agreed to go; what made her accept the invitation was a tipsy moment of curiosity about the man who had fed her whisky all that time ago when they'd found poor little Julie's body together on that blighted Studleigh Common. She wondered if he still smoked the same cheap cigarettes.

'Someone I met over a drink,' she said to Neil. 'It turned out I'd had a . . . a connection with her husband years ago.'

Neil slapped his plump hairless hand against the steering wheel. His hand looks like it's made of plastic, Sarah thought, and in her imagination she saw how Neil would look naked. Like a waxwork in Madame Tussauds, she told herself. Her mind boggled at the thought of his private parts; she visualized him sexless, like a huge doll.

He was saying, 'You mean we're going to dinner with the wife of a man you had an affair with? Does she know? What is she, a masochist? Or does she really, really want to punish him?'

Oh, God, Sarah thought, why did I bring Neil? It's not as if I'm so pathetic I can't accept a dinner invitation on my own without feeling embarrassed because it looks like

I don't have anyone to take. I'd rather that than let people think I'm involved with this dummy.

She had asked Jeff to come with her to the Dillons.

'Who are the Dillons?' he asked. 'I've never heard of them.'

'She's a solicitor,' Sarah said. 'I had a few drinks with her in a bar. It turns out I met her husband years ago when we were looking for Julie.'

'My God,' Jeff said, 'what kind of party is this going to be? I can't come, anyway, there's a Chamber of Commerce do I've got to cover on Saturday night.'

He gave her the half apologetic, half triumphant look he always did when he had no intention of doing what she asked.

'Can't you put it off, Jeff?' she asked. 'I don't want to go on my own.'

As she said the words, she was thinking, I don't think I really want you there, either. It's important to me to meet this man again, and you'll just try to show off in front of him because he was a journalist, and that means you'll try to put me down.

'Well, don't,' Jeff said. 'Make some excuse.'

'I can't,' Sarah said. She thought of Joan, with her sad suffering eyes. 'She'd know I was lying. I can't be rude like that.'

She told herself that she knew Jeff was an unreliable escort. Like Joan's husband had been, he was a reporter on the local paper and he was often called out to work in the evening. But Sarah rarely asked Jeff to do something with her, and she was exasperated that he made so little effort on this occasion.

So, next day in the office, she asked Neil to go with her. She had only herself to blame if she now regretted it.

Sarah thought, I could have gone on my own, but at least Neil can be fun to be with and he gets on with people. I never know where I am with Jeff.

As Neil swung the car round another blind corner she thought, I refuse to think about Jeff now. Soon, but not now. So she tried to be patient with Neil because if she snapped at him he'd think he'd drawn blood in the curious sparring match which was all their relationship really amounted to. 'I didn't have an affair with him,' she said to Neil. 'If you want to know, we were on a search party for a missing child and he found the body.'

Sarah didn't want to tell Neil how close was her connection with that missing child. That was something she still tried to hide even from herself. Knowing she'd been Julie Makepeace's aunt made people treat her differently. As though I'm disabled, she thought.

Neil glanced sideways at her frozen expression and shook his head. 'A fun evening this is going to be,' he said.

Sarah asked herself, why did I ask him to come? I don't even like him, and he's not interested in me.

This wasn't the first time that she and Neil had made up a couple for social occasions. He was an attractive man to look at, in spite of being overweight. His thick, longish hair was bleached gold by the sun, and he had deep-set bright blue eyes which always seemed to be looking at a far horizon. He could be charming, too, and amusing. He wasn't needy, either, which, in Sarah's experience of unmarried men, was a definite plus. She wondered if the secret of Neil's attractiveness for women had something to do with a kind of aura of wealth that he exuded; he even wore his corpulence like a vast mink coat. And most women did find him attractive, even if she didn't particularly fancy him herself. Except, if she were being honest, she did gain something from being accompanied by such an eligible specimen. Particularly on occasions that made her feel nervous, as she did now about meeting the man on Studleigh Common again. And at the very least, having Neil along stopped all those tedious questions about the state of her love life which people otherwise felt free to ask; questions she resented because she was too confused to give a straight answer.

She knew what Neil, for his part, got out of escorting her. When accompanied by Sarah, he could enjoy the coquetry of women who seemed to feel impelled to flirt with him, but without the complication of consequences. Sarah protected him from women's attentions and gave him an excuse for turning them down without offence when they were married to important clients or connections. He was the lone single man in the office, and, with the only other woman apart from Sarah in the firm of architects nearing sixty with twelve grandchildren, he tended to ask for her protection every now and then. So they helped each other out. From time to time, though, Sarah wondered about Neil. It seemed to her that he was scared of any serious relationship with a woman. He played with them like children, the life and soul of the party, but only as long as Sarah was there to say it was time to go home. She wondered what happened when he was alone with a woman. I'll bet he's tongue-tied, she thought, and smiled, feeling a little sorry for him. He talked a lot about women who were what he called 'after him', but it was always about how he'd managed to evade them.

Sarah had asked him once, 'Don't you want to have children?' And he'd said he'd have been happy to have a child, except they grew up and were trouble then. And anyway he didn't want to be involved with a mother, any mother.

That was the only time he'd ever revealed anything about his feelings to Sarah. Or, she thought, probably to anyone else.

'I wish I'd said no,' Sarah said suddenly.

'What's he like, this Angus fellow?' Neil asked.

Sarah wondered why he asked about Angus rather than Joan, who had asked them to come.

'I don't know,' Sarah said. 'I only met him that once. He drank a lot at one time, according to his wife. Apparently he's given up drinking since I met him.'

'Oh, my God,' Neil said. 'A teetotal recovering alcoholic, that's just what I need. He'll either lecture us about the evils of drink or he'll ply us with bad wine to show he's on top of it. What's the wife like?'

Sarah said, 'Are you asking if I think she's available?' She heard how sour she sounded, and was ashamed. Neil was doing her a favour, after all, she shouldn't blame him. So she smiled and said, 'She's sort of glossy, like someone off the tele, but there's something a bit desperate about her. Of course, I'm not a man, but if I were, I'd think the guilt trip wouldn't be worth the effort.'

'You don't like her,' Neil said. He sounded amused.

'I don't have any opinion about her,' Sarah said. 'I don't know her well enough to judge.'

'Want to bet I'll pull her?'

He's like a stupid kid, she thought, he'll try it on with Joan just to prove something to me. It never occurs to him that someone might get hurt.

And then she thought, aghast, does he think he's going to make me jealous? He can't imagine I fancy him.

She remembered Joan as she'd been that night they met, hunched over the table in the wine bar, spilling her heart out to a stranger about the husband she'd fallen in love with and now missed as much as if he'd died years ago. They'd laughed together about the women's magazines' diagnosis of their plight as lack of self-esteem. Feminism hasn't changed anything, Sarah told herself, women still blame themselves for their own suffering.

She said to Neil, 'I hope you do have your wicked way with her. It might boost her self-esteem. Isn't that what all we women need?'

Neil didn't understand sarcasm.

I can't believe what I'm saying, she thought, ten minutes in Neil's company and I sound like a bad psychotherapist.

'All I know,' Neil said, 'most of the women I've got off with I seduced because kissing put a stop to the awful drivel they all talk about their silly feelings.'

Sarah didn't react to this, knowing he was winding her up. It was what Neil did. But she was to remember that exchange with Neil when, later in the evening, she found herself observing Joan with a certain clinical interest, wondering how she struck Neil.

The lost and insecure Joan of the wine bar was gone; tonight she had been masterly in the way she ran the evening, like a conductor teasing a consummate performance from a poorly rehearsed orchestra. And masterly was the word, Sarah thought, there was no feminine vulnerability about Joan that night. She was positively predatory and she'd marked Neil for the kill.

It had started from the moment Joan set eyes on him.

'Oh,' she said, 'it's extraordinary, Neil, you look just the way I used to imagine Angus would look twenty years on. But of course he's turned out quite different to the way I thought he'd be.'

She smiled, mocking her own confused reaction. That smile, Sarah thought, that sudden flash of sunshine fading to habitual sadness, so fleeting you wanted to make it come again to prove the woman could look happy. I bet Helen of Troy had a smile like that, Sarah told herself.

Neil smiled too, clearly not knowing what to say. Sarah could tell that he was not at all flattered by comparison with Angus, then or now.

Joan sighed in a rather theatrical way and seated herself on a sofa beside Neil. 'Ah,' she said, 'there's no harm in dreaming of what might have been.'

During the meal, Joan and Neil talked incessantly about the dullness of their present lives in outer-provincial England. Joan's eyes shone as she told tales of the pleasures of London, and Neil chatted about nights at Covent Garden and the famous people he'd spotted in the Ivy and other famous metropolitan restaurants.

Angus and Sarah said almost nothing, but Sarah had the growing impression that she and he were becoming allies as the others chattered.

'Shall we have coffee on the terrace?' Joan asked. 'I think it's still warm enough, don't you?'

The question was directed at Neil, who immediately got up from the dinner table and went to pull back her chair.

'Lovely,' he said, 'all those stars. Let me help you?'

Angus watched Neil follow Joan out of the French windows and on to the terrace, then he turned to Sarah. 'I don't know about you,' he said, 'but coffee outside is not for me, it's too bloody cold. And if it isn't too cold, there's always a plague of insects. Shall we go into the sitting room and leave them to their illusions of the rustic idyll?'

Sarah laughed and got up. 'You're a man after my own heart,' she said, 'I'm an absolute gnat magnet at the best of times, I hate sitting out on terraces,' and then she felt embarrassed because she thought she sounded too girlie.

She was disconcerted because from the start of the

evening she had been trying to stifle a growing antagonism towards Joan. It wasn't that her hostess had more or less ignored her, turning all her charm and attention on Neil from the start. Sarah found it quite amusing that Neil himself was beginning to look alarmed at Joan's obvious willingness to be seduced by him. But if forty-something Joan was behaving like a sex-starved teenager, that was embarrassing, not really a reason for animosity.

No, Sarah could not put her finger on exactly why she had begun to dislike Angus's wife. It was something about the way the woman treated her husband. In fact, she had scarcely spoken to him. She behaved to him as though he were some awkward aspect of the design of the house, there to trip her if she forgot to remember him, but tedious and annoying. And Sarah resented the condescending way Joan constantly seemed to be trying to enlist the support of her guests in her attitude, as though she was warning them to mind the step.

She tried to remind herself of what Joan had revealed, that night in the wine bar, about her marriage, and about Angus. Sarah had felt sad for Joan then, but now she was sadder still for Angus. She watched the expression in his eyes as he looked at Joan, a look of patient encouragement. He was pleased that the woman was enjoying herself, and Sarah realized that his suffering was far greater than his wife's.

She thought, Joan's got the luxury of feeling angry, and that gives her hope; Angus pities her, he doesn't blame her for the fact that he has no hope at all.

She was suddenly aware that Angus had asked her a question. He repeated, 'There's some brandy if you'd like it?' and she realized that he had asked the question more than once.

She laughed. 'Sorry,' she said, 'I was thinking of something. No, no brandy, thanks. I expect I'll have to drive home.' Then, because she assumed that he would be thinking, as had occurred to her, that Neil was behaving badly, she said, 'I don't mind. It's not as though there's anything between us apart from working together. It's hard for a woman going out alone sometimes, so when I make use of him like this, it's only fair he has a drink.

It's a small price for me to pay, I'm not a big drinker.'

'Who is this man?' Angus asked. 'Neil, I mean.'

'We work in the same office,' Sarah said. She thought for a moment, and then said, 'To be honest, I don't know much about him apart from that. You know, background, where he went to school. That's what you're asking, isn't it? But I've no idea.'

'I just have the oddest feeling that we've met before.'

'Perhaps you have. I'm always forgetting I've met people.'

'I haven't forgotten you,' Angus said. 'I remember everything about you. Except your eyes are grey; I thought they were brown.'

'Well, Neil's probably not all that memorable, not to men, anyway.'

'Oh,' Angus said, 'one of those, is he?'

'The women clients seem to like him, anyway,' Sarah said, and she was ashamed to hear how sour she sounded.

'Do you still work in that architects' office?' Angus asked her. 'You see, I do remember some things.'

'Yes, but I've moved on a lot since then,' she said. 'I love my job now. I do a lot of research for the partners, looking into everything from the history of a site to ancient bye-laws and old building methods, that sort of thing. It's not the usual architects' stuff, I suppose, but the people I work for specialize in rural construction and find it useful.'

'Good for you,' he said. 'I'm glad. I sometimes worried about you . . .'

There was an awkward silence. Politeness demanded she ask about him, and he thought he knew why she didn't want him to spell out how unprofitably he had spent the time since they last met.

So it's that obvious, he thought.

'They must be getting cold outside,' Sarah said at last. 'I'll go and get Neil, it's time we were going.'

'One of the worst things for a drinker about not drinking is knowing how boring you are to talk to,' Angus said. 'It would be a kindness to let Joan divert herself with someone new for a while.'

Sarah looked at him and she wanted to reach out to touch

him, somehow to make him smile. 'I'm not bored,' she said.
'My problem talking to you is I'm afraid I won't be able
to help letting myself go and getting dug into the deep stuff.
You do that to me, I don't know why. And I'm shy about
doing it because we don't really know each other.'

'It's because of the way we met, I think,' Angus said.
'There's a sort of bond. Tell me more about Neil. Is he
your boyfriend?'

'We work together, that's all. He's single, so am I. It's
convenient.'

Why did I say that? she asked herself. I'm not really
single, why did I say I was? And then she thought, is the
wish father to the thought?

'Don't you want more than that? He looks good and he's
amusing and full of life, what's wrong with him?'

Sarah sensed that Angus's interest in Neil was nothing
to do with her, but because Joan had contrived to be alone
with him on the terrace.

So she answered the question she thought he was really
asking.

'As I say, I don't know much about him,' she said. 'I
think there's a New Zealand connection. He joined Savill's
a few weeks after—' She suddenly stopped. Why does
everything I say to Angus come back to that? she asked
herself, then went on: 'Neil's a good architect, the clients
like him. No known vices, as far as I know.' She hesitated,
then went on, 'But it's as though he's playing at everything,
he's not serious. He's like a child.'

Angus smiled. 'You make him sound as boring as I am
without my vice,' he said. 'So he's not your boyfriend?'

'No,' Sarah said, 'I suppose that's Jeff. But he's a bit suffo-
cating. Living with him's like a habit, I don't think he sees
me as a person any more. At least, not the person I am.'

She put her hand over her mouth as though shocked at
what she'd said. 'I don't really mean that,' she said, 'I'm
very fond of him, but . . .'

'Give him an inch and he takes a mile?' Angus suggested.
'I know how he feels. I was like that with Joan, I think.
And look at how that turned out.'

'Don't say that,' Sarah said. 'Please, don't let yourself be so unhappy.'

'Oh, my dear,' he said, laughing, 'what does it really matter? I've got used to being unhappy, I suppose.'

She nodded, a fierce expression on her face. 'It matters to me,' she said. 'I don't know why, but it does.'

He said, 'I don't suppose you've learned to smoke?'

'No,' Sarah said. She smiled. 'Have you learned not to?'

'No, but Joan hates me smoking in the house. I thought if you wanted a cigarette I could get away with it to keep you company.'

'OK,' she said, 'I'll have a go.'

Angus lit two cigarettes at once and handed one to her. Sarah thought, it's like the scene in *Now, Voyager* when the lovers say goodbye. It was because of that, she told herself, that she had tears in her eyes.

Angus inhaled deeply and blew a series of perfect rings which floated lazily towards the ceiling. 'Aah,' he said, 'that's happiness!'

Sarah tried to draw on the cheap cigarette and choked.

'Oh, God,' she said, 'Joan's coming. She must've heard me spluttering.' She sounded like a guilty schoolgirl.

'Think of yourself as a saint, my dear, a martyr to the cause.' Angus hesitated, then added quietly, so that she could scarcely hear, 'One day I hope you won't be afraid to let go and get dug into the deep stuff. I'm looking forward to that.'

Joan came into the room sniffing in an ostentatious way. 'Oh,' she said, 'I'm sorry, Sarah, I didn't know you smoked. I thought Angus had set fire to the place.'

Sarah whispered to Angus, 'Me, too,' she said. And then she said to Joan, 'I'm sorry, I'll put it out at once, it's a filthy habit. I'm afraid I forced Angus into keeping me company.'

She smiled at Angus. She told herself, we're co-conspirators now, him and me.

FIVE

A few days after the dinner party, Angus sat in his study wishing he had something to do. That's what he'd missed most since he'd been fired from the newspaper, a sense of purpose.

He stared out of the window across the garden, where the lawn needed mowing and weeds were mud-wrestling in the flower beds. And beyond that a murky dark-grey bank of rain cloud seemed to rest on the hedge dividing the cottage grounds from open fields.

Why don't more housewives go mad? Angus asked himself. Millions of them trapped at home alone every day with boring chores they don't want to do and nothing to surprise them. And yet most of them aren't mad.

He turned on the television, and stared pointlessly at the screen. This is too stupid, he thought, I'd *rather* mow the lawn.

He was about to turn off the TV when he caught the end of a local newsflash.

'Oh, my God, no, not again,' Angus said aloud.

A child was missing. A fifteen-year-old girl had quarrelled with her friends at a club in Hunsteignton and set off alone to walk home. She had never arrived. Her friends had tried to phone her but her mobile was switched off.

A young, smiling girl's face appeared on the screen, a photograph taken at some party where she was evidently having a good time with other teenagers who had been carefully cut out of the picture. There was a sense of unreality about the lost girl then, as though she had been caught in a private game of *Let's Pretend*.

On screen, her mother, scarcely able to speak, told a reporter her daughter was a happy, lovely girl, loved by everyone. She pleaded with her child to come home, she wasn't going to be in any trouble, they just wanted her back with the family where she belonged.

Since early morning, according to the report, police had been searching the area close to her home. They were making house to house enquiries. No stone would be left unturned in the effort to return the girl to her family.

Angus told himself, I'll bet she was done up specially for that photograph, she won't look like that in real life. She's made up to look older than she is, like a woman, and she's just a child. And then he thought, that's just the journalist in me, always suspicious; she may really look like an eighteen-year-old, lots of these girls do. Some bastard's fancied the eighteen-year-old she said she was, and abducted her and killed her, and it's not fair, that's not who she is, she doesn't even get to die as herself.

How can this sort of thing happen, he thought, how can anyone do something so terrible to anyone, let alone to a child? And for what, after all?

Angus turned off the television, but the missing girl remained in his mind after the screen went blank. He thought of Sarah and that horrible day on the common when he and she had searched for her missing niece.

He wanted to protect Sarah; he wanted her to know about this new case, but not find out from strangers. Knowing about Julie, one of her friends could easily blurt out something that would bring it all back.

Don't be a fool, he told himself, you're a stranger. How do you think you can make it easier for her to be reminded?

And then he thought, she can put the phone down on me if she doesn't want to talk to me, but if she does, if it would help, I should do it.

That very morning, though, he'd been reminded how inept he was with women. At breakfast, Joan had made it more than obvious that he had nothing to say that she wanted to hear. They had had what she would call a huge row. He hadn't said more than a few words but she had ranted at him about what he thought and what he wanted and what he did, and how he never listened to her or cared how unhappy she was.

And then she'd said, 'You don't want me to be happy, do you?'

He refilled his coffee cup and held up the percolator, offering to pour for her. She ignored him.

'I do, more than anything I do, but I don't know how to help you,' he said helplessly.

'You can't, I don't want help from you. I've met someone else and he does make me happy.'

Joan gave Angus a frightened look then, as though she had said more than she'd intended and was scared he might fall to pieces in front of her.

She leaned across him to help herself to toast. 'Angus, I'm sorry,' she said, 'I know you're hurt. But you must know it's been over for us for yonks.'

'You've never said anything,' he said.

'Oh, I stuck it out because I know how much you depend on me. But now I've met a man I love.' There was a moment's pause and then she added, 'And who loves me.'

Angus considered some dramatic gesture of protest, anything to shock her out of doing something she would regret. But then he thought, what's the point, I've nothing to say to her.

He asked, 'Are you going to tell me who he is? Someone at work?'

Joan glared at him. 'Is that all you've got to say? How can you just ask me that, as though you're checking a fact in a stupid newspaper story? You're so cold, Angus, you don't have any feelings. You're not a real man, you've turned into a zombie.'

Angus surprised himself by wanting to laugh. He thought of all the times he had deliberately held himself back to give her the freedom to think or feel what she wanted without trying to influence her, or spoil things for her. Sometimes he'd longed to put his arms around her or tell her how much she meant to him, but then he'd been afraid that she would think that he was stifling her and instead he had found something encouraging to say.

'I'm sorry,' he said simply.

She'd screamed at him then. 'Is that all you can say to me? Doesn't it mean anything to you that I'm in love with another man and now I can scarcely stand to be here with you any more, you great grey slug monster parasite of the world?'

He did laugh then, and she burst into tears.

He said, 'I've no intention of trying to hold on to you if you want someone else, Joan. I want you to be happy.'

She stopped crying and he handed her his handkerchief so that she could dry her eyes.

It seemed to Angus as though she were rehearsing a part in a play and he was hearing her lines. She seemed to miss a cue, but he had no idea what she expected from him.

And then she had suddenly slipped out of her role and become her normal self.

'Oh, Angus, what a mess,' she said. 'I can't believe how much I love him, or how much it hurts.'

He said nothing, waiting for her to go on.

'He doesn't love me,' she said, 'not the way I feel about him. It's Neil Carver.'

'Neil? That fat fellow who came here with Sarah Makepeace?'

Angus was astonished. He tried to remember something memorable about Sarah's friend, but he couldn't. There was nothing about the man who'd come to dinner to interest any woman, not as far as he could see, anyway.

'I don't know what you're thinking of,' he said, 'are you menopausal?'

Joan looked angry, but when she spoke it was with the voice of patient reason. 'You see, you're doing it again. Neil would never say something like that. He's so sympathetic, he understands me, who I really am,' she said. 'And he makes me laugh. We have fun, he makes everything fun. You and I haven't had fun like that since the first year we were married.' She sounded sulky then.

'I scarcely talked to him, I wouldn't know,' Angus said, and despised himself for his appeasing tone.

Joan got up and began to gather her things together to go to work. 'You know,' she said, 'one of the things that first attracted me to him was that he reminded me of you. In the old days, the way you used to be.'

'Gawd,' Angus said, 'I hope that's one of your insults. I wouldn't want it to be true.'

Joan didn't take offence. She wasn't listening to him, she

just went on, 'Oh, it's not looks or anything like that. Being with him takes me back to when you were funny and charismatic and full of confidence.'

'Young, you mean? But he's not young, is he, he's about the same age as us, isn't he? Or do you mean he's a bit backward? You know, immature?'

That's probably a truth too far, he told himself.

Joan opened her bag and rifled through it for her car keys. 'Age is nothing to do with it,' she said firmly. 'He's what the young man I fell in love with would have been if he hadn't turned out to be you.'

Angus was still trying to unravel what she meant as he heard the front door slam behind her.

I need a drink, he thought, I really need one. He asked himself, why am I so inept with women? Except it wasn't all women, just those with whom he was emotionally involved. It had always been the same. Whenever he cared about a woman, he seemed to cast a kind of blight over the relationship, unable to provide their love for him with anything to feed on. And yet he did everything he could to hold them; he never stopped caring, he tried to understand them and give them what they wanted. But he was never sure what that was, he never had been; not, at least, until they made it clear that they wanted only to be free of him. They'd all reached that point, sooner or later. Joan had stuck it out much longer than any of the others. And he still couldn't work out why, what he had done to bring about the change in their feelings for him.

Psychologists, he thought, would probably blame his mother's rejection when she abandoned him at birth. But Angus could not blame her, whoever she was. God only knew what nightmare she'd been going through then, how frightened she must have been. He couldn't blame a woman he had no knowledge of. He wasn't even interested in who she was. It didn't matter now.

Angus opened the cupboard under the sink with its array of bleach and cleaners and polish. He found the bottle of whisky where he'd left it behind the washing up liquid. Thank God, Joan had never found this one, he thought, that's one of her virtues, really, she's never been one for housework.

He sat back at the breakfast table and poured the remains of his coffee into Joan's cup. Then he filled his empty mug with Scotch and drank it down.

That's better, he thought, feeling the lovely fiery liquid slowly creep through his body. Joan probably hadn't meant what she said, she was just letting off steam. She'd get over it.

And why should he be sorry for himself? As a child he'd never felt unloved, whatever that might mean. He'd taken love for granted, just as he'd never questioned that Mum and Dad were his parents. What the hell did it matter, anyway? It wasn't as if he'd been aware early on that he had been 'rejected'. He hadn't been told that he was adopted until he was in his mid-teens and Mum had needed a new kidney. He'd offered to donate one of his and then Dad told him that he had no genetic connection with her. Dad had been upset, but Angus wasn't. He had always thought of his adoptive parents as his real Mum and Dad. As far as he was concerned, motherhood lay in carrying out the job, not in refusing to take it on. It was Mum who'd made him what he was. Never for a moment had he felt he did not belong with the couple who brought him up as their own, part of their simple, protected life in Otterbrook, where Dad went off to Exeter every day to work in an insurance office, and Mum belonged to the local WI and came to the school sports day and bought him Meccano sets and toy pistols for his birthday. Where she was, there was his home; and she had always been at the centre of the circle of whitewashed thatched cottages huddled into the hillside overlooking the river that was Otterbrook. Perhaps if she hadn't died so soon, Angus thought, if she'd been there when I first started to go out with girls . . .

But she had died, and he'd never been able to ask her about women and what they wanted. It didn't matter now.

Everything had changed after she was gone. Most of the cottages in the village were second homes now, owned by rich city people who came down on occasional long weekends and jammed the narrow lanes with their glossy 4 x 4s.

I've changed, too, Angus thought, I couldn't live in the village now. I'm the outsider, living in this remote cottage well away from anyone, but it's no life for Joan. She'd be better off in Exeter, or going back to London.

Angus found himself unwilling to grapple with his feelings about Joan's breakfast bombshell. He couldn't even muster any curiosity about what would happen next. Was she going to move out and live with this Neil? Or what? Was it going to make much difference to his life? Or not?

He asked himself, what does it matter, really, compared to what the parents of that missing girl must be going through? Something like that would change their lives for ever; even if their child is found safe, things will never be the same for anyone in that family again.

Sarah would know how that felt, and this new nightmare must bring it all back for her. Angus wondered, would it help her to know I understand that? She could talk to me if she needed someone. Or am I just being an idiot? Has she got over it and put it behind her and the last thing she'd want is some old man ringing out of the blue to stir it up again?

The doorbell rang then, and he wanted to ignore it. But he couldn't. The sound was intrusive. Angrily, he drained his Scotch and went to answer it.

Sarah stood on the doorstep. When the door opened, she was turning away to return to her car.

'Sarah,' he said, 'I was just thinking about you.'

She looked strained and anxious, finding it hard to meet his eyes.

'I wasn't sure if I should come,' she said. 'I didn't know if you'd want to see me.'

'I was just debating whether I should call you,' he said. 'I'd just got out the Dutch courage.'

She followed him into the house. 'I didn't know if you'd heard,' she said. 'I thought someone should warn you.'

He was puzzled, then remembered Joan and her toast-muffled revelation about Neil.

'About that friend you brought here?' he asked. 'Don't worry about it. Joan's love life has been an accident waiting to happen for years, if it hadn't been Neil it would have been someone else.'

Angus felt that he was sounding too flippant. He said, 'I want her to be happy and I know she's not happy with me.'

They were in the kitchen, and Angus filled the kettle and started to make coffee to keep his hands occupied. Sarah leaned against the table and watched him.

'I didn't mean that,' she said, 'I don't know anything about Neil, or Joan. I came because I thought you would be feeling bad about the missing girl they're looking for. I heard it on the radio this morning and suddenly I felt this great compulsion to talk to you.'

Angus put down the kettle. 'I thought you might think I was intruding if I rang,' he said. 'I'm so glad you came.'

Sarah took off her coat and sat down at the kitchen table. He poured her a small whisky and a larger one for himself.

She said, 'I nearly lost my nerve. The doorbell sounded so loud, I panicked. I was on the verge of running away.'

'Well, I'm glad you didn't,' he said. 'I'm glad you're here. Except now I don't know what to say.'

She smiled. 'It's weird, really. We hardly know each other, and yet there's this one intimate thing between us which is like a bond that'll last for ever.'

'I know.'

'Every year since . . . every year at that horrible time, when it's brutally cold and everything seems frozen to death, I think of Julie and that day we found her, and although the memory is horrible then I think of you, and it's like the first sign of spring, as though in spite of everything there is warmth in the world.'

'Wow,' he said, 'that's more or less what I wanted to say to you, only I wouldn't ever have had the guts to say it. Or been able to find the words, come to that.'

They grinned at each other, both embarrassed but oddly comforted.

Sarah said, 'I wanted to say, this isn't like the other time, not really. It's horrible, but it's not like Julie. What was so awful then was that a child was violated, innocence defiled.'

He shook his head. 'But surely that's what's happened, isn't it? She's just a bit older, that's all.'

'According to Jeff – my boyfriend, Jeff Acres, who works for the newspaper here – this girl was on drugs and she's been cautioned for soliciting.'

'God,' Angus said, 'that makes it worse, in a way.'

'You can't say that . . .' Sarah was outraged.

'Don't you see, this makes us all responsible, not just some pervert. This girl's dead because of the society we've all created for our children to live in.'

'That's different from Julie,' Sarah said. 'You could say this girl set herself up to be a victim, Julie didn't.'

Angus understood that she feared that the new atrocity would dilute what happened to Julie. 'I'm sorry,' he said, 'I'm so sorry, but for me it is different. Julie was killed by a monster, no one could do anything about it, we can't feel personally guilty. But we all had a hand in what this other girl became, and that's what put her in the way of her death. We could have done something to change things so this didn't happen.'

She was staring at him, not wanting to try to understand, and he knew he couldn't really explain the guilt he felt about this latest outrage.

'Tell that to my sister-in-law,' she said.

And then the doorbell rang again, on and on. Then someone hammered on the door. A man outside shouted: 'Police, open up.'

'What the hell . . .?'

Sarah followed as Angus went to open the door.

There were several uniformed policemen in the front garden. In the driveway, Sarah's car was surrounded by police vehicles.

Angus pulled Sarah behind him as two plain clothes cops brandishing warrant cards swept him aside and charged into the house.

'What is this?' Angus shouted at them. 'What do you think you're doing?'

He was acutely aware that he was wearing his old dressing gown and that his legs and feet were bare. He felt horribly vulnerable. It seemed to him that his home was being invaded by rampant prehistoric tyrannosaurs who set about laying waste his belongings, ignoring his puny protests.

'Angus Dillon?' said one of these policemen, the one who seemed to be in charge.

Angus nodded uncertainly, as though he was not sure of his real identity.

The policeman stepped forward. 'I am arresting you on suspicion of the murder of Tara Davidson,' he said.

'Who? Who's Tara Davidson?' Angus managed to whisper.

The policeman carried on talking regardless, but Angus didn't hear anything he said.

'She's the missing girl who was found murdered, the one on the news,' Sarah said. Her voice was hoarse and her terrified face looked grey. She slumped against the wall as though she could scarcely stand.

Angus ignored the policemen and spoke to her. 'They think *I* murdered that girl?' He sounded dumbfounded, unable to decide whether to laugh or be angry at the overwhelming bad taste of what must be the policeman's humour. 'Seriously?' He appealed to Sarah, 'How can they possibly think that?'

SIX

Joan tried several times to telephone Neil at his office, but each time she was told he was on site out of town and wouldn't be back until late afternoon. She could hear an increasing note of exasperation in the voice of the woman who answered the phone, and, in the way of lovers on the tremulous brink of committing themselves, Joan began to wonder if the girl had been told to put her off.

Surely not, not when at first she'd been quite open about when Neil was expected back? But then, when Joan rang at four thirty, Neil had not returned, and she detected a definite hint of sly triumph in the girl's voice.

'You said he'd be back,' Joan said, trying to stifle the note of pleading in her own voice.

'We expect him back,' the girl said. 'Do you want to leave a message for Mr Carver?'

'No,' Joan said. Bitch, she thought, she's laughing at me.

She couldn't bring herself to ring again, so as soon as she could get away from work she drove to Savill's offices in the High Street and parked opposite the entrance. At least this gave her the feeling she was doing something positive.

It was now well after six, and the traffic was lighter. She stopped on a double yellow line, hitching the car up on the pavement and hoping that the traffic wardens had finished their shift. Most of the shops had closed, but there were still lights on in the offices. Savill's, though, was an ultra-modern building which faced the street behind impenetrable smoked glass, so it was hard to tell if there were people there or not. Joan told herself that if Neil had got back late after being out all day, he would still be at his desk. There'd be things he'd have to deal with before going home.

She dreaded seeing Neil and she dreaded not seeing him. She had to tell him that she'd told Angus about their relationship, but she dreaded his reaction much more than she had worried about what Angus would say. Neil might be really angry with her. Oh, my God, she thought, I've gone too far. Why did I do it? She felt sick, and her palms were sweating as she clutched the wheel. Part of her wanted to flee, go to a bar and get drunk, pretend she'd never said anything to Angus, but she couldn't do it. She had to wait.

Neil came out at last, amongst a group of people with the unmistakable stamp of office workers in transition between their daytime selves, moulded in the corporate image, and the out-of-hours individuals they would become by the time they reached home. Neil stood out among them because he didn't look like that. There was no aura of the employee about him.

All those grey people must hate him, Joan thought, just by being there he's rubbing it in that they're wage slaves. And then she asked herself, am I like them, a colourless work-obsessed nonentity grabbing on to a free spirit like some sort of adrenalin junkie?

She started the car, preparing to drive off before he saw her. She'd been an idiot, a clingy self-pitying nuisance who'd given that horrible girl on the phone and, no doubt, her giggling colleagues, an excuse to sneer at 'Neil's new stalker'.

The sudden sound of the engine caught Neil's attention and he saw her. He waved and smiled, and she knew that he was pleased to see her and that she'd made herself miserable all day for no reason. Thank God, she thought, just being with him is like being plugged into a power socket, I can cope with anything.

Neil waved at the group of colleagues who were breaking up to make their way to the station or the multi-storey car park behind the shops in the High Street. They don't hate him, Joan thought, he's a life force, he gives them a reason to want to get up for work in the morning.

Neil leaned in through her open car window and aimed a kiss at her.

'Hey, Joan,' he said, 'how's things? What's the light of my life doing in this neck of the woods? I thought you'd still be buried under a weight of legal tomes.'

'I tried to ring,' she said. 'There's something I've got to tell you. Can we go somewhere to talk?'

He walked round and opened the passenger door of the car and got in, leaning across to kiss her lightly on the cheek. She was suddenly very conscious that she scarcely knew him. Where can we go? she asked herself. We've only ever spent time together in bars and cinemas and restaurants, we've never really been alone.

'I was out all day,' he said. 'We've got problems with a new project and I was meeting the clients on site to try and sort something out.'

Joan bounced the car off the kerb and joined a line of traffic stopped at pedestrian lights outside a supermarket which was still open.

'Where are we going?' she asked. 'Where can we go?'

He gave her a quick look and something in her face seemed to warn him not to suggest the pub or a nearby Indian restaurant.

'My mother's away for a few days,' he said, 'we could go to my place. Turn right at the next roundabout.'

She didn't tell him that she knew the way to the house on the outskirts of town where he lived with his mother. She'd looked up the address and driven past it several times over the past weeks. She'd even tried to imagine herself living there, as she'd slowed down to crawl past in the dark, trying to see some sign of what his life was like behind the lighted windows. The curtains were always closed, so she'd learned nothing, but she had felt comforted by the connection with him.

'Left at the next junction,' Neil said.

They scarcely spoke on the way. She liked the silence between them, companionable and undemanding. Their previous flirtatious, teasing conversations in bars and restaurants were fun, and were part of why she had fallen in love with him, but now this contented silence between them introduced a new intimacy which made her feel happy.

The house had been built between the wars, an ugly red-brick family home with a central gable and a large bow

window overlooking the drive and the road. Now it didn't
look ugly to Joan, it seemed like home.

She followed Neil into a carpeted hallway leading round
the staircase to the kitchen at the back of the house.

'How long have you and your mother lived here?' she
asked. She wondered if it was because of all the years living
with Angus in the old cottage that this house seemed to her
to have an unlived in feel. There was something clinical
about its neatness and a certain cold aura of professional
cleanliness. Joan pictured Neil's mother as an old-fashioned
nursing sister, stiff with starch, daunting and demanding, a
woman for whom no daughter-in-law would ever be good
enough for her only son.

And then Neil handed her a glass of wine, and she saw
his smile and she knew that she had only imagined the
whiff of Jeyes fluid.

'An old uncle left it to my mother years ago,' he said. 'I
came here to live with her when I left New Zealand. That
was about six years ago. I've thought of moving on, but
after all, she's getting older, and it suits us both for me to
stay. Or it has so far,' he added, giving Joan a suggestive
look which made her smile because she liked the idea that
now he'd met her, he had a pressing reason to find somewhere of his own.

She smiled, and he put his hand on her arm and said,
'Shall we go and sit somewhere more comfortable?'

For a moment Joan thought he was suggesting they go
upstairs, and she was embarrassed at her disappointment
when he led the way into the sitting room. Here the decor
was magnolia and the sprawling sofa and armchairs were
covered in beige. A set of coasters printed as Union Jacks
offered the one bright touch of colour.

Joan sat on the sofa, hoping he would sit beside her, but
he placed himself opposite on one of the armchairs.

'Well,' he said, 'spit it out.'

'I told Angus I'm in love with you,' she suddenly blurted
out.

It was as though Neil hadn't heard what she said, the
way he seemed not to react at all. Joan stared at him,

afraid that she was going to have to repeat her bombshell.

Then he said, 'Are you?'

She had expected him to say something quite different and she didn't understand what he was asking.

'I told Angus,' she said. 'About us.'

'Yes,' he said. There was a pause and then he asked, 'What happened then?'

Joan thought for a moment and finally said, 'Nothing.'

She met Neil's blank eyes and suddenly she wanted to laugh hysterically. 'Nothing happened.'

'Well,' Neil said, 'I suppose that's Angus for you.'

Joan stared at him. 'Is that all you can say?' she asked.

I'm ridiculous, she thought, I've done something momentous today and it's as though no one takes me seriously. Even I'm beginning to believe that nothing really happened.

Joan was getting frightened. She felt trapped in a limbo where she had no control. When she'd told Angus that she loved Neil, and then when she told Neil that she had left Angus, it seemed to her that she had shut off the past and opened the door to a changed future. But neither Angus nor Neil seemed to have understood. They appeared to hear what she said, but it was as though the three of them were playing parts on the stage, and nothing she had to say bore any relation to their real lives.

'Neil, I think I've left him,' she said.

'You don't sound very sure,' he said, and though he looked sympathetic she felt he was teasing her. He was like a small boy poking a caterpillar he'd collected to see what it would do.

'I have, I've really left him,' Joan said. 'I've told him it's over between him and me. I said I'm with you now.'

'Did he believe you?'

Neil's tone revealed only an almost prurient curiosity that struck Joan as oddly detached. It reminded her of the way Angus had been long ago when he was a young and enthusiastic reporter grilling some victim for a story. She was suddenly furiously angry with Neil. She could scarcely stop herself lashing out at him. 'You don't love me, do you?' she said.

'Darling, of course I love you,' he said. He came to her and took her glass and put it down on one of the Union Jack coasters on the glass-topped coffee table, and then took her in his arms.

Joan's tears were hot against the skin of his neck. She was whimpering, 'You won't let me down, will you? Please, Neil, don't leave me now.'

Neil put her gently away from him. 'Darling,' he said, 'of course I won't let you down. I'm just worried for you, that's all. I think we should book you a hotel for tonight and then try and sort something out tomorrow.'

'But can't I stay here?'

'It's too much of a risk,' he said. 'My mother's due back any time. She could just walk in on us, and that, my precious, would put the cat among the pigeons.' He leaned over and kissed the tip of her nose. It was still damp, like a dog's.

It's no good, Joan thought, I still feel like I'm being embraced for the umpteenth retake by Cary Grant and I keep getting it wrong.

After a few moments Neil put her gently away from him. 'Now come on, sweetie, this won't do. Everything's going to be all right. We've got the house to ourselves for a while at least, I'm a terrific cook, and the night is young. So what's to cry about?'

'Oh, Neil,' she said, and her voice wobbled as she started to smile through her tears, 'I love you so much.'

'That's better,' he said. 'Now finish your drink before the glass stains that awful coaster, and come and talk to me while I cook.'

Joan picked up her glass and followed him to the kitchen. Suddenly she felt happy, happier than she'd ever felt in her life before. At last, she thought, I've got a future to live.

SEVEN

Sarah imagined she could still hear the sound of police sirens long after the cars had gone. It had been over an hour now since the cops left, and she hadn't moved from her place in the hall where Angus had put her behind him when the policemen rushed into the house.

They had taken Angus with them when they went. For questioning, they said.

He had gone with them without protest, and Sarah could see in the eyes of several of them that they took this as some kind of admission of guilt. An innocent man would surely have more to say in his own defence.

But Angus hadn't said a word. Not after that hideous moment at the start when they burst in, and the one in charge had been positively drooling with excitement when he said he was arresting Angus Dillon on suspicion of murdering Tara Davidson, and Angus had ignored them and asked her who that was, and how the police could possibly think such a thing.

And she had told him who he was accused of murdering, and suddenly something inside Angus seemed to break and he was helpless to stop himself, he unravelled like a piece of knitting and he started to laugh. He laughed and laughed until even the triumphant policemen looked disconcerted, and the plain clothes Chief Inspector didn't try to hide that he was telling himself to put this prisoner on suicide watch. He wasn't going to have this conviction complicated because the murderer established a case for pleading insanity.

Two uniformed men took Angus out to a waiting car, and as they half-dragged him away he turned and, still gasping, said to Sarah, 'The perfect end to a perfect day!' He was still laughing.

The plain clothes Chief Inspector lingered in the hall, dispatching men in baggy white boiler suits to search the house. He had a fatherly look about him, Sarah thought, as if he was worried all the time. She guessed he was in his forties, but there were grey strands in his dark hair, and deep lines around his eyes.

'Where did you find the girl's body?' Sarah asked him.

'Why? Are you thinking of giving your boyfriend a false alibi?' the Chief Inspector said.

'My boyfriend is the senior reporter on the local paper,' Sarah said. 'I just want to know and so will he.'

The Chief Inspector seemed embarrassed. He coughed, then said unwillingly, 'She was on the common. She'd been strangled.'

'And why have you arrested Angus?'

'We've reason to suspect he killed her.' The Chief Inspector was frowning and his voice was flat.

'How can you be so sure?' Sarah asked at last.

'It's my job,' the Chief Inspector said.

He gave her a frigid smile and she wanted to hit him.

He was trying to get away from her. He said, 'We've taken your name and address. If we need to talk to you we know where to contact you.'

'If you think I'm going to just walk away and leave this, you're wrong,' Sarah said, but even she could hear that her bravado sounded querulous.

The Chief Inspector dismissed her with what he may have thought would pass for kindliness. 'I'm surprised at any woman defending him,' he said. 'In my experience women are dead set against child killers.' He looked at her with revulsion, as though she had admitted she was implicated in Angus's crimes.

Sarah tried not to show how cowed she felt by this man. The white boiler suits of his team didn't help; she seemed to be in the grip of something beyond human control. She said, 'I'm sure most women, as well as quite a lot of men, still believe someone is innocent until he's proved guilty, even a child-killer.'

The Chief Inspector turned away and walked out of the house.

EIGHT

'What do you think of child-killers?'

Angus, sitting on a hard plastic chair at a table in the interview room at the police station, stared at the senior of the two officers facing him. He had been in charge of the men who'd barged into the cottage and accused Angus of killing the girl on the television. The other man was a sergeant. A real brute, Angus thought.

'I don't think I've ever met one,' Angus said coldly. 'I'm choosy about who my friends are.'

He knew at once that he had made a mistake. He saw a purplish flush rise up the Sergeant's hefty neck, as though someone was filling him with blackberry juice. The man might be a heart attack waiting to happen in a few years' time, but now he was no joke. Stop it, Angus told himself, don't make smart remarks. You're only doing it because you're nervous. They've made a dreadful mistake and they'll find that out before long and let me go, but till then don't make enemies of them . . .

'Because in here we have a very low opinion of filth like that,' the Sergeant said. 'In here we think men like that, who'd harm a kiddie, are the scum of the earth.'

Angus suddenly remembered that far-off day on the common when he'd found the poor broken body of little Julie, and how he'd felt as he tried to protect Sarah from seeing her lying half-hidden by the rotting trunk of a fallen silver birch. He'd sat there on the bleak common smoking one cigarette after another, hearing the first tentative twitters as nervous birds stirred again, and he had almost wept with the intensity of his hatred then for the man who had killed the child. For the first time in his life, he'd wanted to kill someone.

He and these misguided policemen were on the same side.

'No one would argue with that,' he said. 'It's the worst there is.'

Oh, God, he thought, what wouldn't I give for a drink now? Or even a cigarette.

'Good, we agree about that,' the senior policeman said. He looked worried, as though he wasn't sure he could control his Rottweiler of a sergeant if Angus persisted in his attitude of defiance. 'So I hope you're going to make things easy for yourself and not try our patience by telling us you didn't do it. My name is Detective Chief Inspector Gifford and this is Detective Sergeant Knowles and we're going to ask you a few questions. Do you confirm that you have decided not to exercise your right to have a solicitor present?'

'I don't need a solicitor,' Angus said. 'I know I'm innocent, and I want to get this over with as soon as possible and get the hell out of here, so let's get on with it. What I want to know is why you are questioning me at all. What do you think I can tell you?'

'Oh dear,' Sergeant Knowles said, showing the two prominent front teeth that had made his childhood a misery because they made him look like a fat rat. 'All this could be over very quickly if you told us the truth and confessed.'

He must've been bullied as a kid, Angus thought, no wonder he became a policeman.

He told himself, I'd confess to anything they want if they'd only give me a drink.

He turned to Chief Inspector Gifford. 'Tell me about this girl,' he said. 'Who is she and where does she come from?'

'So it was just random, was it?' the Sergeant asked. 'You just happened to see this kid and you took your opportunity? Why her, Angus? What was it about her?'

'Where did you kill her, Angus?' Chief Inspector Gifford said. He sounded sad, as though he was asking these questions more in sorrow than in anger.

'Cat got your tongue, Angus?' Sergeant Knowles said.

Angus ignored him. He suddenly felt how oppressive the bleak interview room was and how hostile the two policemen were. The senior one might look more tractable, but he was just as hostile. Angus knew from the old newspaper days that they were baiting him, trying to make him lose his temper and lash out at them. They're looking for an excuse to beat me up, he told himself, they don't care if I'm guilty or not, they want to take out their hatred for child-killers on someone.

'I didn't kill anyone,' he said to Chief Inspector Gifford.

'Did she offer you sex for a lift home?' Sergeant Knowles said. 'Is that why you took her up on the common? And then she didn't want to go through with it so you forced her and suddenly you'd killed her? Is that what happened?'

'No,' Angus said. 'I don't know what you're talking about.'

'Perhaps you didn't mean to kill her?' Sergeant Knowles said. 'Men like you who use child prostitutes like Tara are looking for something a bit extra, I suppose. If you weren't a pervert, why would you go with a kid like that, a fifteen-year-old kid. Even if she was a tom. After all, you're a married man. I've seen your wife around the court, she looks like a bit of a goer. Or is she getting her rations elsewhere?'

'Leave my wife out of it,' Angus said, struggling to control his anger.

But the Sergeant wouldn't stop. 'And then there's the daytime bit on the side, the young woman at your house with you today,' he sneered. 'What's the matter with you, you a sex addict or something?'

Angus was about to explain about Sarah and then he thought, what's the use? There's no point in dragging her into this. These yobs wouldn't understand anyway.

Their air of having some secret knowledge intimidated him. Instead he smiled at the Sergeant and said nothing.

Chief Inspector Gifford said, 'You don't seem to realize the seriousness of your situation, Angus. Tara Davidson was a young girl of fifteen with her whole life ahead of her and now she's dead.'

'What kind of future is there for a fifteen-year-old who's already on the game?' Angus said bitterly. 'What was it, drugs?'

'You think she's better off dead, do you?' Chief Inspector

Gifford said. 'Is that why you killed her, to save her from a life of degradation, or even from losing her soul? Are you some kind of religious fanatic, Angus?'

'Of course not,' Angus said. 'A young girl like that, it's a tragedy, but then so's her life a tragedy, obviously. As a society we should be doing much more to help children before they get into trouble and these horrible things happen.'

God, he thought, hearing himself, what a pompous nerd I sound.

He said quickly, 'But if she's a druggy and on the game, what makes you suspect me? You can't have any evidence against me, I've never seen or heard of Tara Davidson before. Why aren't you questioning her clients as suspects, not me? I don't even know where she was found.'

Sergeant Knowles leaned forward, humouring him. 'You know the place quite well, according to your girlfriend. She told us that she'd been there with you before, you'd taken her there once a few years ago. Tara was like the other victim, she was found on the common. A pretty place, they say, among silver birch trees, where the ground's easy to dig. Her killer had made an effort to bury her.'

Angus shook his head. 'I haven't been there for years,' he said, 'not since . . .'

'Not since you found the body of Julie Makepeace, is that right?' Chief Inspector Gifford said. 'Tara's body was lying close to where Julie was when you found her.'

'They say murderers always return to the scene of their crime, don't they?' Sergeant Knowles said.

'Who says that?' Angus asked. 'I'll bet it was a policeman browbeating some poor innocent suspect by pretending to have evidence against him.'

Damn, he thought, I shouldn't have said that. There's no point in making them angry. 'I need a drink,' he said. 'Is there any chance of something to drink?'

'In a moment,' Sergeant Knowles said. 'Just a few more questions now and then we'll send someone to get you a tea from the canteen. The sooner you tell us what we want to know, the sooner you can have a drink and a cigarette.'

Tea? Angus thought, I need much more than a cup of bloody tea.

Knowles pulled a packet of cigarettes out of his pocket and took one out and lit it. He inhaled slowly, loudly, then went on, 'What did it feel like, Angus, after you'd killed that young girl? Did it make you feel like a big man? Did you cut notches on one of the birch trees for your victims?'

'Where were you on the night of Saturday tenth last?' Chief Inspector Gifford asked.

'I don't remember for sure,' Angus said. 'At home, I should think. I almost always am.'

'Can anyone vouch for that?' Chief Inspector Gifford asked. 'Your wife, perhaps? Or did you have people in?'

'Yes, yes, my wife can corroborate that,' Angus said. And then he thought, Saturday night, she's been going out on Saturday nights. 'If she was in, that is,' he added.

The Chief Inspector caught Angus's sudden doubts.

'You're sure about that?' he said. 'You haven't remembered you were somewhere else? If so, say so now.'

'No,' Angus said. 'As far as I remember I was at home. I can't remember if my wife was.'

Sergeant Knowles gave a great mocking sigh. 'Ah,' he said, 'Marriage à la mode, doesn't that say it all? I wish I couldn't remember when my wife wasn't at home on a Saturday night.'

'We'll check it out,' Chief Inspector Gifford said.

'Is that when you think this girl was killed, the tenth?' Angus asked.

'You ask a lot of questions for a man in your situation,' Sergeant Knowles said, abandoning his friendly familiarity.

'Sorry,' Angus said. 'The reporter in me surfaces when I'm near cops.'

'That Saturday night's the last time we've got CCTV footage of her. She was coming out of a club in Hunsteignton at about one thirty a.m.,' Chief Inspector Gifford said.

'Well one thing I know for sure, I wasn't in Hunsteignton on that Saturday night or any other Saturday night,' Angus said. 'And if I remember my court reporting days rightly, you have to prove I was, I don't have to prove I wasn't.'

The two policemen were silent.

'OK,' Angus said, 'so tell me what you think you've got, because I know you haven't. What are you going on? Car tyres? footprints?'

He thought, I can't think clearly, I need a drink.

'It's not as simple as that,' Chief Inspector Gifford said, staring at his big hands which lay like ribs of beef on the table between him and Angus. He said, 'We're just trying to piece Tara's movements together. You see, Angus, we may not be able to prove you were in this place or that with her, or exactly when you were with her. But we know you were. We may not know exactly when she died, or even where, yet; but it's a fair bet you probably had sex with her before she died, and we're quite sure that you were the man who put his hands round her neck and choked the life out of her and then stubbed out a cigarette on her dead body.'

Angus jumped to his feet. He was really angry. Sergeant Knowles leaped up and came round behind him to hold him back before he could attack Chief Inspector Gifford.

But Angus had sat down again. 'I need a drink,' he said, 'I can't think without something to drink. And a cigarette. You're pushing it, you haven't even charged me.'

Inspector Gifford and Sergeant Knowles leaned back in their chairs as though they had been practising synchrony for effect.

Angus said, 'Is that the best you can do . . .'

For the first time since Angus had met him, Chief Inspector Gifford smiled. 'The best I can do?' he said. 'No, I can do better than that. I can prove it.'

'You're living in a dreamworld,' Angus said, 'how can you possibly prove a lie like that?'

'DNA, Mr Dillon,' Gifford said. 'Your DNA from the National Database is a perfect match for samples we took from the scene of crime where we found the girl's body. There's no margin for error at all.'

NINE

The house where Neil Carver lived with his mother Nellie was a fairly undistinguished villa built in the thirties in the open country two miles or so outside Hunsteignton.

After she had inherited the house from an old uncle who died intestate, and when she returned to England from New Zealand, Nellie had planned to sell the house. She was a practical woman, unsentimental. The villa was perfect for a prosperous professional family, with a big garden for children to play safely, within easy commuting distance of Hunsteignton, and close to shops and schools and nice middle-class activities like riding schools and tennis courts. There'd be no trouble selling it and she could do with the money. She had left Neil and his stepfather, Vince, far behind in Auckland, and she intended to make a new life for herself in England.

But Nellie liked the house. She liked the feeling it gave her that she had done well for herself. It was better than anything her parents had ever achieved, in spite of the social pretensions which they used as an excuse for throwing her out as a teenager for bringing shame on them. Nellie had never forgiven them for that, and she was still sorry that they had not been around to witness her triumph. It never occurred to her that if they had been alive, it would probably have been her father, not her, who would have inherited the villa as a closer relative to the beneficent uncle. Anyway, she liked the solid red-brick no-nonsense look of the villa and the straightforward boxy structure softened by the gable at the front, with none of the fussy nooks and crannies of most of the other much older houses in the area. She decided to stay.

That was almost twenty years ago. Since then she had practised as a vaguely-defined alternative therapist, offering remedies extracted from plants to relieve the frustrated and disappointed middle-aged women who flocked to take advantage of her listening ear and the gentle promise of her scented oil massages and mysterious herbal teas.

She had modernized the house and re-enforced the clinical simplicity of its design. She changed its name from Acacia Villa to Heart's-ease House, which was more in keeping with her trade. She had worked hard, too. She'd rotavated the half-acre of lawn which had been the pride and joy of the previous owner, and laid down beds of herbs and medicinal plants from which she now concocted her own oils and tinctures.

Sometimes the clients who visited Heart's-ease House were disconcerted by the contrast between the clinical cleanliness of everything in the house and Nellie herself, who was one of those women who seemed to have given up on her appearance many years ago. She was a tall spare woman with ruddy skin crazed by years of exposure to sun, wind and rain. Her untended, greying hair was tied in a knot on her neck, but as the day went by it rebelled and broke loose. Often there were stray leaves and the odd stalk caught in the rough tangles.

Nellie's hands, though, were the tools of her trade; big, strong, spade-like hands shaped like a mole's. Some of her nails were always broken, and stained with earth and plants from her work. As a masseuse, though, she had a magic touch which drew even reluctant clients to return to consult her time after time.

And then one morning a few years ago, Nellie had answered the door and Neil was standing on the step. He said he had left New Zealand for good. Nellie had never really found out why. He'd got a life there. He'd graduated from the School of Architecture and Planning at the University of Auckland and started on what looked like a promising career, too, with a good job working for a firm of land developers.

He'd told her some story about Vince getting married again and having a new kid, and how Europe was a more exciting place for an architect to be. Nellie concluded that

Neil, for so long the only child, resented Vince's new baby and took off to regain the solo spot with his adoring mother. She told herself this was absurd, Neil was a grown man, but nevertheless it was the only explanation she could think of.

Nellie wasn't particularly pleased at first. She knew that she had never been able to be the kind of devoted, uncritical mother Neil had wanted her to be. From the time he was a small boy she'd feared for him. He was bullied, and he was always the wimp other children taunted him with being; he'd cried too easily, he was afraid of everything, he clung to her and wouldn't let her go. She tried not to, but she despised him just as the other children did. Only too often she asked herself how she had produced a child like this; she, who prided herself on her grit and toughness. And she had nightmares about what would happen to him, how he would survive on his own when he grew up.

Her fears faded after he left school. Vince had been good for him, he had learned to survive. Nellie, her fears allayed, lost interest. But after Neil had been with her at Heart's-ease House for a while, she began to enjoy having a personable young man about the place. In his early days at the villa, Neil talked of moving out and finding a bachelor flat in the centre of town. Nellie had encouraged him. But Neil had got himself a good job with Savill's the architects; his social life was so busy she scarcely saw him in the evenings, and it seemed silly to insist that he wasted money providing himself with the expense of a flat he would scarcely use. Time enough for that when he found himself a nice girl and wanted to get married. So, though the two of them occasionally made passing reference to the place of his own he would one day find, neither thought it was really going to happen. And they were both happy with that.

Indeed, Neil was thinking of exactly that as he parked his car in the drive outside the house. He realized that he now had a problem with Joan Dillon. He was concerned about what he was going to do to put off the silly woman, who so suddenly seemed intent on becoming much more a part of his life than he had ever intended.

Where did I go wrong with her? he wondered as he let himself into the house. He had taken it for granted, when he'd escorted Sarah to that awful dinner party at the Dillon's cottage, that Joan was a married woman of long standing who might be up for a little mild flirtation in daylight hours, or in crowded restaurants, or at the theatre, but would never risk anything more intimate. That's why Neil liked married women. He was always in control. Or, at least, his mother was. His mother was a kind of third party on every date. He could always say that she needed him at home; she got nervous if he wasn't home before the pub closed; she'd made him promise to be home for her visitors. It suited Neil and his married women fine. But then there was Joan.

And now the silly woman had left her husband and spoiled everything. Neil didn't know what to do. He wasn't used to women behaving in this unilateral way, making decisions for themselves which now threatened his lifestyle. He didn't know what Joan meant when she said in that breathy way she talked to him that she loved him, that she wanted nothing more than to be with him, that they must be together.

Many women had told Neil that they loved him. He had said the same thing to most of them. But Neil wanted nothing more than to be forever in the early stage of falling in love. Not for him the next steps of getting to know her, getting to know all about her. He wanted to repeat endlessly the initial first excitement of intrigue with different women; that constituted all his interest in them. He was not an imaginative man and it never occurred to him that other people might not feel about love as he did. He wouldn't have cared if it did. He had no intention of hurting anyone. And, because none of his women had ever really loved him, he never had. But now this silly Joan threatened to ruin everything because she'd played the game without, apparently, ever learning the rules. He thought she must be psychologically disturbed, and he was wary of anything like that.

Neil locked the car and walked towards the house. He'd left for work early that day, now it was late, but there was a light on in the hall. Nellie must have come home. He hadn't her to be back. He thought she was returning

tomorrow. I should've known, he told himself, she was
bound to come back early to check up on what I've done
wrong. He knew that she would have noted the lipstick on
one of last night's unwashed wine glasses, the washing up
he'd left in the sink, and disapproved of the make-up stains
on the tissues Joan had thrown into the waste paper basket
after she'd had her cry. Well, too bad if she does, Neil
thought, except he knew Nellie would be pleased, she'd
start asking arch questions about his girl and was this The
One, and he didn't want that. He knew Nellie wanted to
see him married. In no time she'd be talking about grandchildren if he didn't nip her speculation in the bud.

'Is that you Ma?' he called as he opened the front door
and stepped into the lighted hallway.

Nellie came out of the door to the kitchen, which overlooked the garden at the back of the house.

'I got an earlier train,' she said.

Neil kissed her. 'What was the matter?' he asked. 'Get
bored with your own company?'

Nellie tried to laugh, but she was ashamed that her trip
away had only reminded her of the loneliness of her life
with Neil.

She thought, do I love him? And if I do, why don't I like
him? He's rubbish company, that's why, it's like being with
a spoilt child all the time, why can't he grow up?

She made an effort and told him: 'I made supper in case
you weren't going out.'

'Oh,' he said, 'I'll stay in. I thought I'd one more night
of freedom to put the house straight, so I hadn't made plans.'

Nellie wondered, is he trying to apologize? He didn't
usually bring his women back to the house, but then, she
was always there herself as a deterrent. Nellie had been
startled at the signs that he'd had a girl there. That was
unusual. She took it as a declaration that this relationship
was serious, that at last he was thinking of settling down.
Perhaps he is growing up at last, she thought

This thought made her feel much more cheerful.

'Let's eat off our knees in front of television,' she said.

'Sure,' he said. He was surprised at her sudden gaiety,

but at least television would stop her interrogating him about Joan.

They had finished eating, and Neil had persuaded Nellie to leave the washing up till later, when an item came on the news that the police were questioning a former journalist in his forties about the death of teenager Tara Davidson, whose body had been found on the common close to where the murdered schoolgirl Julie Makepeace had been discovered some years ago. The man police had arrested had been involved in the earlier search for the murdered schoolgirl Julie Makepeace.

A smudged photograph of Angus appeared on the screen.

Neil recognized Joan's husband and tried to hide his shock by starting to say something flippant about how police photographs of suspects always made them look guilty. But before he could speak, he heard Nellie gasp and give a muffled cry.

Her face had gone very white. Her big hands on the arms of her chair seemed to be in spasm, and her mouth sagged open as though her jaw had suddenly broken. She looked like a bad sculptured version of the figure in *The Scream*.

Neil jumped up. 'What's the matter, Ma?'

She shook her head, raising her hands to push him away.

He sat back down again. 'You looked as though you'd seen a ghost,' he said. 'What happened?'

'I need a drink,' she said. 'Whisky.'

In the dining room, as he set out the glasses and poured whisky for them both, he thought, I saw a ghost too. Angus looked like something conjured up by a guilt trip out of *Hamlet*. I know why I might think like that, because of Joan, but why Ma? Why did seeing Angus have such an effect on her?

He took the drinks back into the sitting room. Nellie was sitting as he had left her, staring at the screen where some hospital drama had started.

The colour came back into her face and she looked more like her normal self as she drank the whisky he gave her.

'What was it?' Neil said. 'What was it about that man?'

He expected her to make light of it and pretend the picture

of Angus had triggered some sort of unwanted memory in her subconscious. But she said nothing.

'I know that man,' he said, 'at least, I know his wife. I've met him. He's harmless. He can't do anything to you.'

'You *know* him?' Nellie said. 'You've met him? Face to face?'

'Yes,' Neil said. He was puzzled by her insistence.

'And nothing struck you about him?'

'What, that he could be a child murderer? Honestly, Ma, if he is, it doesn't show when you meet him.'

'That's all?' she said, and frowned.

Neil joked: 'His wife said I reminded her of him years ago when she first met him,' he said. He thought if he was flippant it might help her get over her obvious fear. 'I couldn't see it myself, but perhaps women are better at spotting these things.'

Nellie started to cry.

'Ma . . .?' Neil didn't know what to do or say. He had never seen her weep. She's not the type, he told himself, she's always hidden her feelings. Or perhaps, he thought, she doesn't feel much, she's emotionally cold. He felt that perhaps he should touch her, put an arm round her heaving shoulders, or pat her hand. But he couldn't bring himself to do it.

Then Nellie cried, 'Oh, my God, how can I ever forgive myself?'

TEN

Angus thought, last time I was in a police cell they at least let me keep my own clothes.

Now they'd taken away his belt and his shoes, and made him put on a hideous garment made of some kind of paper.

He told himself that they were out to humiliate him, take away any dignity he might have been able to cling on to because he was still an innocent man who had not been proved guilty. They were putting on the pressure to force him to confess. As far as they're concerned, he thought, I'm guilty as hell. Nothing's going to change their minds about that, not even when they finally have to drop their case.

As far as he could remember, the last time he'd spent a night in a police cell was years ago, in his drinking days, when he'd got into a stupid fight with a barman who'd refused to serve him and he'd been locked up for being drunk and disorderly. There'd been no paper clothes then, and they'd let him go first thing in the morning.

Someone in a cell further up the corridor started to shout and swear in some language Angus didn't recognize, until he remembered how he himself had tried to communicate in English with lips and tongue almost anaesthetized with alcohol. He's talking drunk, Angus thought, drunkenness has a language of its own. He wished that he himself had had enough to drink to carry on a conversation with his unseen neighbour. It's a universal language, he told himself, and I've forgotten how to speak it.

Someone snapped back the metal grille in the door of his cell. A bleary, greyish eye stared at him, as though accusing him of something he was yet to do, then disappeared.

Angus sat hunched against the wall on the hard narrow bench, which a small pillow, apparently made of concrete, and a single grey blanket indicated was his bed.

What the hell happened, he asked himself, how did I get here? What's going on?

'I'm Angus Dillon,' he said aloud, 'I'm married to Joan and I've lost my job and I'm pretending to write a novel, and that's about it. What do these cops want with me?'

So who is Angus Dillon? he asked himself.

There wasn't much to say, really. He was just an ordinary bloke, the normal run of the mill product of an overcrowded English secondary school, one of hundreds of thousands of people who live unspectacular lives doing the things men of their sort do – earning a living, drinking in the local pub, watching television, supporting the county cricket team and pretending to share his boozing friends' interest in Yeovil Town Football Club. And then he thought, it's not much to brag about, but at least I've never deliberately hurt anyone or done any real harm, so why am I here? Who do they think I am?

And that was the point, wasn't it? He had lost a grip on the reality of his own identity. Angus wondered how Joan would describe him. Would she come and tell these policemen who he really was, that he couldn't be the pervert they wanted to make him? But who *was* Joan's Angus? A disappointed and self-centred man who smoked and drank too much, who had betrayed her hopes for their life together; a man who avoided the important issues between them, and took flight in the face of her needs and feelings? A failure she was forced to dislike in order to keep a hold on any hope she had for herself; except he wouldn't *be* disliked, he wouldn't stand and let her hate him, he simply slipped away and closed the door behind him.

She thinks I'm a drunk, Angus told himself; she thinks she has to protect herself against me. I gave it up but she still saw me as a drunk, and so from then on I suppose I drink without enjoying it because that is what she expects. As far as she's concerned, I've got my own priorities – I had drink and now there's cigarettes, and, if she's not totally given up hope, she thinks I've got my writing. She probably believes I don't care about her.

He suddenly felt almost overwhelmed by pity for the

Joan he'd married. I never meant her any harm, he thought, and I've ruined her life.

He asked himself, is that me, the real me?

He found himself remembering nights out in the pub at the end of his newspaper shift, long nights when there was nothing to go home to, and the barmen and the regulars and most of all the drink in the Fleet Street bars filled his life, closer than family because he saw more of them and had good times with them. Almost every night someone would get maudlin; there'd be tears and regrets and sympathy. But that was always yesterday. Every day would start afresh, there were no recriminations, no memory of what they'd said and the secrets they'd revealed. They accepted each other for what they were. And what was that? We were drunks, he thought, pure and simple, it was the wonderful camaraderie of drunks.

He thought, if any of those old drinking mates came back into my life, they wouldn't even recognize the ordinary, sober, unremarkable Angus Dillon I am now. It was a sad thought.

And what about the policemen who accused him? He asked himself, who do they think I am? A child murderer, an abuser of young girls, the most despicable of all killers? That's how they see me. They are so sure, they have no doubts at all about it.

He thought, they're far more certain of who I am than I am myself. I don't recognize myself in the creep they see me as, but I don't know how to change their perception of me. I haven't got any form of moral identification about the real me. I can't argue with their confidence. It's my word against theirs about who Angus Dillon is, and I'm not even sure myself any more.

The grill snapped back again, and another eye stared blankly at him; it was a dark-brown eye, this time registering him not as a man, but as a physical pattern sitting upright on the bed. He was still there, he hadn't tried to harm himself or even move, the correct shape was not distorted. That's who I am, Angus thought, a shape, that's all.

He closed his own eyes because the naked overhead light

in the cell hurt them and his head ached as though his brain had been beaten up.

Against the red glow of his closed eyelids, it seemed to him that he saw the face of Sarah Makepeace, full of life, smiling, happy, strong. She doesn't judge me, he thought, she hasn't got some preconceived notion about who or what I am.

Sarah's image faded as hot tears welled up and spilled down his cheeks, catching on his unshaven chin. He felt a wave of affection for her, and gratitude. She knew better than he did himself the man he was. Sarah was his witness and he wept out of stupid happiness that he was no longer on his own.

ELEVEN

Sarah had a positive phobia about not being late. This was often irritating for other people because she always arrived too soon, when politeness demanded she be a little tardy. It was also irritating for her because, arriving too early, she had to sit around waiting for the appointed hour. She tried all sorts of psychological tricks on herself to break the habit, but it was no use. During the course of a year she accumulated many wasted hours this way, hours she could have put to better use.

This was why she was sitting alone in a corner of the Crown and Garter, the one and only pub in the village of Otterbrook, resigned to passing the hour or so before she had agreed to meet Joan at the Dillon's cottage.

It had seemed an enchanting place; an L-shaped thatched building with roses climbing over the white walls and a terrace looking down at the shallow amber river overhung by trees.

Sarah stared at the half-pint glass of beer she didn't want to drink and wished she'd stayed in the car instead of coming in to the bar. But she couldn't muster the energy or the will to get up and march out of the place now.

She wasn't sure, though, how much longer she could stop herself from making some sort of scene and taking issue with the group of locals who were luxuriating in a discussion about Angus Dillon's arrest for murdering a child prostitute. There was no doubt about it, they insisted, Angus had been charged. Talk about kangaroo courts, Sarah thought, as far as they were concerned Angus was already charged and convicted, and if the government had the sense to bring back the death penalty for child murder, he'd have been executed already.

Sarah heard that the police had closed their investigation, they were so sure they had their man. The landlord of the Crown and Garter had been told so by a man whose teenage daughters were best friends with the daughter of the Chief Inspector in charge of the case. The police had DNA evidence of murder and of rape, and there were several unsolved cases of missing girls which they were now adding to the pervert Dillon's tally.

Sarah had tried all day to get information from the police. No one at the station would speak to her. She knew they were not revealing anything to the public. But now she found herself having to resist believing what she was hearing, these people in the pub were so convinced of what they were saying.

She rang the police again on her mobile. All she wanted was a scrap of real information which could keep these bloodhounds at bay. But each time it was the same: 'We have your name on file, Miss Makepeace, and if we need to speak to you in this connection we know where we can contact you.'

What's the point of finally getting through to a human being when he turns out to be the prototype of the bloody answering machine? she asked herself.

And now listening to Angus's friends and neighbours relishing what was happening to him was making everything much worse. Thank God he can't hear them, she thought, it's making me suicidal, seeing how these people are turning on him, God knows how he'd feel.

'There's DNA evidence,' an untidy middle-aged woman in a Barbour was saying. 'That's what they're saying. On the body. You know what that means, don't you? Semen. It's open and shut.'

'*In* the body, I heard, Mrs Thwaite,' another woman said in a penetrating whisper.

'I've always thought there was something odd about Angus,' the landlord said, licking beer froth from his fat lip. 'There was something not quite right about him, I always thought. He wasn't your normal run of social drinker, for a start. I said to Betty when he first came in, "You mark my words, Bet, that man's got something on his conscience." Didn't I say that to you, Bet?'

He appealed to his ageing baby-faced wife, who looked as though she was still growing out of her toddler's clothes. She nodded, admiring his prescience.

'His wife's got a fancy man in Hunsteignton,' a military type leaning on the bar was saying. 'That tells you something, I always think, when a chap can't hold on to his wife. Something wrong in the bed department, I say.'

'But raping and killing little girls, that's too awful to think about. They should bring back the death penalty for men like that.' The speaker, a young woman of about Sarah's own age with a plump pink face and blonde hair, was in tears. 'And to think . . .'

Sarah hated her; hated them all. How could they condemn Angus like this, unheard. They were so sure he was guilty, this man who had for years, until yesterday, been one of the regulars gathered with them at this bar several evenings a week. They'd heard rumours and there was no doubt in their minds. And, Sarah thought, they were making up the lies that condemned him as they went along, to justify themselves.

Mrs Thwaite, the untidy middle-aged woman in the Barbour, ordered another round of drinks. 'You know,' she said, 'if my memory serves me right there was a previous occasion . . .'

'There was, you know,' the landlord's wife said. 'Wasn't there? Years ago. Something happened up on Studleigh Common. Something to do with Angus and a young girl.'

The military man screwed up his face with the effort of thinking. Then he thumped the bar, making the newly-filled glasses jump.

'That's right,' he said. 'By Jove, it's coming back. There was a child missing and the village turned out to search the common. Angus found the body.'

'Odd that when everyone's searching, he was the one to find her,' the landlord said. 'Almost as if he knew where to look.'

'Well, now we know he did,' Mrs Thwaite said. 'And that wasn't the only young girl who's gone missing in this area. He's probably killed a whole string of them.'

'If I ever clap eyes on him again, they won't have to string him up,' the military man said. 'Castration's too good for scum like that.'

Sarah couldn't explain what was happening to her. She wanted to leap to her feet and scream abuse at them, making them understand that she knew Angus was innocent. But at the same time she was overwhelmed by an oppressive apathy, so that all she wanted to do was shut her eyes and allow herself to sleep.

She caught sight of the clock above the bar. She was now late for her meeting with Joan, and that made her nervous. She took her glass to the bar and put it down.

She said quietly to the untidy woman in the Barbour, 'It was my niece whose body Angus found on the common, I was with him when we found her, and I know he didn't kill her. The DNA evidence was because he smoked a cigarette to calm himself down. And as it happens I was with him when the police came this time and asked him to help them. He went with them because he wanted to help. Perhaps you should be more careful with your unfounded accusations.'

Mrs Thwaite stared at her. Sarah met her eyes and was shocked at their glazed, unfocussed look. She's half-cut, Sarah told herself, she scarcely knows what she's saying. But it doesn't matter, she's still certain that Angus is a killer.

'That's all very well, young lady,' the woman said in a drawling tone as unfocussed as her eyes, 'but what you don't seem to realize is that Angus Dillon is a married man.'

Sarah turned to walk away. As she opened the door on to the street, she heard the military man saying, 'Can you imagine the cheek of that girl, interrupting a private conversation? Well, eavesdroppers never hear good of themselves.'

Poor Angus, Sarah thought as she got into her car, what kind of life can he have had around people like that?

TWELVE

Joan had been surprised when Sarah rang and asked to talk to her. She'd telephoned at an ungodly hour, too, just after seven in the morning. The girl must think it was urgent to call so early.

Joan wondered now why she hadn't asked Sarah what she wanted to talk about. At the time she'd assumed that the woman carried a torch for Neil and resented losing him to an older woman, but now she thought that wasn't likely. Neil had sworn to Joan that there had never been anything between him and Sarah, and she believed him. Sarah wasn't the sort of woman men like Neil fell in love with, she thought, she was far too unsophisticated and normal. She's like an organic vegetable, Joan told herself, Neil's taste is more exotic.

So what did Sarah want? Joan had assumed that the dinner party where Sarah had introduced her to Neil would be the end of any possible friendship between her and the young woman, to whom she'd revealed too much over too many glasses of wine one night when she'd been particularly low. At the dinner party, she'd felt that Sarah didn't even like her much. It was Angus she seemed to get along with.

Also when Sarah rang Joan hadn't had her wits about her. In fact, she had only just got in. She'd spent the night at a grim roadhouse-style hotel just off the A30. It was meant to be the first night she and Neil would spend together. Joan shied away from admitting even to herself that it had been a total and rather embarrassing failure. She'd hoped that Neil might have let her spend the night with him, but he hadn't asked her to stay. Joan shied away from admitting to herself that she was disappointed.

From the start, things went wrong.

She ordered champagne. She hadn't even noticed that it tasted more like Asti Spumante. But Neil had.

'They're taking the mickey,' he said. 'They think they know why we're here and they're banking on us not making a fuss. God, I feel like reporting them.'

'Who would you report them to?' Joan said, trying to lighten his mood. 'This isn't the sort of place which has any stars to lose, is it?'

She tried to persuade him to come to bed, but he pretended there was something he particularly wanted to see on television. But there wasn't really, and he kept flicking from one channel to another in an irritable fashion.

Joan went over and tried to sit on his lap.

'Neil, what is it? What's wrong?' She ran her fingers through his thick blonde hair.

He smiled at her, like a cat enjoying being stroked. 'Nothing's wrong,' he said. 'Except I know how much you wanted everything to be perfect.'

'It will be, I promise it will,' she whispered. 'I think we're nervous because being so much in love is new to both of us.'

'It's not perfect timing, is it?' he said.

'Your mum, you mean? Don't worry, darling, everything's going to be fine. She'll get used to the idea. Surely she's going to be pleased that we're happy and in love.'

Neil grimaced. 'She won't, you know. She'll be jealous as hell. She'll think you're out to take her place.'

Joan wanted to say, 'For God's sake, Neil, you're a man in your forties, you don't need your mother's approval,' but of course she didn't. Instead she said:

'She's your mother, I could never take her place, even if I wanted to. It's not as if I'm going to try to stop you seeing her when we get a place together, is it?'

'All the same, I want to break it to her gently, you see that, don't you?'

Joan didn't respond to that, because she couldn't think of how to say she didn't see that at all. But Neil didn't notice her hesitation. He said:

'Darling, how would it be if you didn't leave Angus just yet? A few more weeks and we could find somewhere we could live together and by then my mother could get used to the idea of me leaving home. What do you say?'

Joan stared at him, aghast. 'No, oh no,' she wailed. 'Think what you're asking. Have you any idea what it would be like for me to go back to being in that house with Angus while we wait for you to pluck up courage to tell your mother we're going to live together?'

'I know, my love, I know.' Neil took her hand and kissed her fingers. 'Do you think I want to waste any more time? But it might be for the best in the long run. A little while longer, that's all I'm asking, and then . . . well, we've got all the time in the world.'

'How do you figure that?' Joan demanded, pulling her hand away.

Neil seemed to be choosing his words carefully. 'You haven't met my mother, have you?' he said.

'No. So?'

'If we're not careful she could get awkward and make things difficult for us.'

'Oh, don't be absurd. She's your *mother*, for God's sake, and you're a grown man, you're over forty. How can she make things difficult?'

'She can make out she's ill so she needs looking after; she can try blackmail, cutting me out of her will unless we have her living with us; she can spread rumours about us and damage our reputations. We're both in professions where a client's good opinion matters . . .'

Joan laughed. 'Rumours about what, for heaven's sake?'

'Oh, she'll find something,' Neil said. 'And if she doesn't, she'll make it up.'

He sounded resigned, as though he had suffered at his mother's hands before and knew the harm the old woman could do to get her own way.

Joan did not believe him. 'Neil, this is your mother you're talking about. How can you say such things? You're making her out to be some kind of monster.'

'No. No, I didn't mean that. She's getting old, she's afraid of being left alone, that's all. She was in New Zealand a long time, and she hasn't made many friends here. She's lonely, and she's getting on, and she relies on me, she really does. I'm all she's got. She'll come round. I just need to prepare the ground, that's all, so she doesn't feel she's being threatened.'

Joan began to think she herself might be making too much of a fuss. She could wait. She'd told Angus their marriage was over, he would understand that she and Neil were planning a new life together, there was no point in making things difficult when they had all the time in the world. So she nodded, and said, 'So you want me to stay put at the cottage till then? I don't know how Angus is going to take that, but I suppose I've been living unhappily with him for years, I might as well hang on a little longer when we're going to be so happy soon.'

'I like Angus, you know,' Neil said.

'I don't think he thinks much of you,' Joan said. And then she thought, that's unfair, Angus didn't say he didn't like Neil, he just seemed to think he wouldn't make me happy. Poor Angus, I suppose in his own way that's what he's always wanted, for me to be happy.

'Well, I don't suppose he does, in the circumstances,' Neil said, 'but as soon as we're over all that we'll get on like a house on fire, I'm sure we will. He's my kind of bloke.'

Joan looked at him in wonderment. Was he serious, or was it some kind of elaborate mockery? Joan knew that Angus would never be Neil's kind of bloke whatever the circumstances. Angus saw Neil as superficial and unctuously charming, a man without integrity or passion, a self-centred and unprincipled clown.

The opposite of him, Joan thought, Neil is everything he isn't. She touched Neil's face with caressing fingers. She wanted to tell him that she loved him, make him say he loved her. But she stopped herself. She thought, I don't think I could bear it if he didn't say he did. I don't want to know if he doesn't feel the same way about me as I do about him.

But in case Neil was serious about somehow not falling out with Angus, she offered a sop: 'One of the things I love about you is that you remind me a bit of how he used to be,' she said. 'You look a bit alike, in a way, around the eyes, and the shape of your head . . .'

Neil laughed. 'We're about as alike as Jack Sprat and his

wife, I'm afraid,' he said. 'Angus looks like a marathon runner and I'm more of a rugby front row prop, don't you think?'

'Oh,' Joan said, 'it's just something about the way it used to be with Angus . . .'

Neil pulled away from her.

'Darling,' he said, 'I can't go through with this. Not here, not tonight, it's all too sordid.'

Joan folded her arms over her breasts like an outraged chamber maid in a silent movie.

'Oh, Neil,' she wailed, 'please . . .'

'It's no good,' he said, 'this horrible warm fizz and talking about my bloody mother and Angus, it's put me right off . . .'

'But we can't just walk out,' she said, 'They made me pay in advance.'

'Oh, God,' Neil said. 'You see what I mean, it's sordid. You stay here if you want, but I'm off. When we do this, I intend to do it properly.'

And he had put his jacket on and was gone.

Joan sat there open-mouthed, flabbergasted. She had nowhere else to go, so she stayed. Later, she'd tried to ring his mobile to show there was no ill feeling, but he didn't answer. She tried again first thing in the morning, but his phone was switched off. She went home.

She'd expected Angus would already be up and about at the cottage. She called his name as she opened the front door, but there was no reply. She tried to convince herself that she was not surprised.

When Sarah called, she expected it would be Angus. But then she remembered that he thought she'd left him. Where was he? Angus never went out much. He had nothing to do in the outside world that she could see, so where was he? Joan disliked the empty feel of the house. It felt curiously menacing. She'd never noticed it before. She had never expected that her appreciation of the cottage as home had involved Angus being there. Without him, it now felt unfriendly. She was frightened by the loss of something she was used to taking for granted.

He probably went on some sort of bender after yesterday, she told herself. He was upset enough. She thought, it must've been the hell of a shock when I told him I'm in love with Neil. And when I said I'm leaving him.

Did I say that? she wondered. Had she actually said she was going to live with Neil? She hadn't meant to go that far. She and Neil had never actually discussed setting up home together. Anyway, Angus scarcely noticed if she was home or not; he wouldn't turn her out.

She wondered if she should offer Sarah something to eat. Why didn't I tell her to come round later, after normal people have supper? she asked herself. I was the one who told her to come at seven thirty, it was a way of giving myself time, but it was stupid.

At exactly seven thirty she heard Sarah's car stop outside the house. So she's one of those, Joan thought, one of those bloody people who are always on time.

For the first time she wondered about the girl, what she was really like. Anally-retentive, anyway, she told herself as she opened the door, hoping that what she was thinking didn't show in her smile of welcome.

But Sarah didn't notice. She looked tired and scared, and her voice was strained.

'What's wrong?' Joan said at once. She thought, it can't be Neil, she wouldn't tell me if anything happened to him.

Sarah put up her hands in a gesture of helplessness. 'Have you checked your messages?' she said.

Joan had heard the same note of strain in the voices of guilty defendants about to go into court.

'Sarah, sit down,' she said, in her firm detached lawyer's voice. She pulled the girl forward into the house and shut the front door firmly behind her. Then she ushered her into the living room and on to the settee. 'Now tell me what's the matter?'

'I was trying to ring you all last night,' Sarah said, and her voice sounded panicky, as though she was rationing her breath so she'd have enough to say what she had to say. 'When I did finally get you this morning, they were there and I couldn't tell you . . .'

'They? Who are they?' Joan could hear the note of irrita-tion in her own voice. The girl was almost hysterical and they were getting nowhere. She wondered if she should slap her.

But Sarah managed to gain a little control. 'The police,' she said. 'I wanted to tell you what's happened before they talked to you. If I blurted it out in front of them, I thought it would make it worse for Angus.'

'*Angus?* What's Angus got to do with it? Has something happened to Angus?'

Sarah looked at her then as though she was suddenly seeing Angus's wife for the first time. Something shocked and fearful in Joan's face helped Sarah pull herself together.

My God, she thought, she thinks he's guilty of some-thing. She believes he's done something awful, she's expecting what's coming.

But Joan was suddenly catapulted back to the days when Angus was drinking, when even an unexpected knock on the door almost always presaged some sort of crisis and a summons to the police station or the hospital. Joan's concern, after all these years, was complicated by a kind of remem-bered excitement at the prospect of a drama.

'What's he done?' she asked Sarah.

Sarah was shocked at what she saw as Joan's detachment. Angus was living a nightmare and his wife was behaving like one of those horrible people at the pub.

Sarah shouted at her: 'Didn't you even wonder where he was? He's been with the cops since yesterday. He's been charged with murder. Murdering a child. The police aren't even investigating properly, they're so certain.'

Joan went very white and sat down suddenly in an armchair by the open fireplace.

'No,' she said, 'no, it can't be true.'

'Of course it's not true,' Sarah yelled. Then she said more quietly, 'Of course it's not true, but they believe it is and that they've got the facts to prove it.'

'Facts?' Joan said. 'What facts?'

'DNA,' Sarah said. 'They say his DNA matches samples from the . . .' – she couldn't say the word body – '. . . the scene of crime.'

'Oh, my God, not again?' Joan said. She spoke almost under her breath, and Sarah couldn't make out the words.

She suddenly wanted to attack Joan, shake her until she could force some positive emotion out of her. 'What's the matter with you?' she hissed at her. 'Don't you understand? He's an innocent man and this awful thing is happening to him and he's completely helpless. You're his wife, you've got to do something. You're a lawyer, you can help him.'

Sarah burst into tears.

'It's a mistake,' Joan said, 'a mistake like last time. They had to admit it then. They will this time, when they realize it's a mistake.' She put her hands over her face as though her eyes couldn't bear the light. 'Why does this keep happening to him?' she moaned.

Sarah, still shuddering with sobs, heard the braying tones of a middle-aged woman in a Barbour proclaiming at the bar of the pub, 'if my memory serves me right there was a previous occasion . . .'

Joan stood up. She went to a sideboard and took out two glasses and a bottle of whisky.

'Here,' she said, 'drink this. We need it.'

She handed Sarah a full glass and swallowed the whisky in the other at a single gulp. She refilled it, then returned to sit in the armchair.

'I don't have to tell you,' she said, 'it was a relative of yours, wasn't it? They got the DNA from a fag end Angus smoked. They practically accused him of the murder then.'

Sarah nodded. 'I didn't know that at the time,' she said, 'but you told me when we first met. But this is different, surely? Joan, they're so sure of themselves, it's scary.'

'They'll be out to justify themselves, that's all. They were made to look idiots last time and they'll never forgive Angus for that.'

Sarah tried to tell herself that Joan was simply trying to whistle in the dark.

She said gently, 'But it wasn't Angus who made them look like idiots, was it? They went off at half-cock, that's all.'

'It'll be the same this time, you mark my words,' Joan said, and smiled at her.

Sarah understood then that Joan would not or could not help Angus now.

'All the same,' she said coldly, 'what are you going to do? Somebody's got to help him.'

Joan stood up, dismissing her. 'They'll realize soon enough if he's innocent,' she said. 'There's nothing I can do to help. Angus wouldn't want me involved, anyway.' She ran her fingers through her hair, pushing it back in a gesture that made Sarah think she was deliberately shaking off the past.

'I might as well tell you, if Neil hasn't already,' Joan said, 'I've told Angus I'm leaving him. He knows it's all over between us. Neil and I are in love.'

Sarah, who liked Neil in spite of herself, and knew him well, wanted to laugh out loud and tell Joan what a fool she was. But that wouldn't help Angus. Joan would have to find out for herself that Neil was always in love with some woman, the same way he loved dry martinis or old St Trinian's movies. Maliciously, Sarah allowed herself to hope that he would teach Joan Dillon a painful lesson.

'Well,' she said, getting up and moving towards the door, 'at least I felt I had to tell you before the police catch up with you asking questions.'

Joan followed her out. 'Thanks for coming to let me know,' she said. 'But I'm sure there's no reason for you to worry. They'll realize they've made another mistake.'

'Perhaps when they do you should sue for compensation this time,' Sarah said as sarcastically as she could. 'That might stop it happening again.'

THIRTEEN

Neil's mobile phone rang. It was Joan. Automatically, he turned it off. He had nothing to say to Joan; it was Nellie he must deal with.

After that agonized cry of hers, 'How can I ever forgive myself?' he had tried to reassure her.

'It's not your fault, Ma,' he told her. 'You can't blame yourself because someone kills a child. You don't even know that man.'

And then Nellie had let out a kind of wail like an abandoned dog. 'He's my son,' she howled, 'that man's my son.'

Neil snapped his phone shut and put it in his pocket.

'No,' he said, 'he's not your son. I'm your son.'

Nellie, white-faced, her wild hair medusa-like, whispered, 'He is too. That man's your brother. Your brother Angus.'

There was a long silence. Then Neil said, 'You'd better tell me what's going on.'

He could feel his stomach knotted around a core of foul-tasting fear inside him. He thought, how come something intangible like fear has a taste? But it did, a sour acidic flavour he had to swallow hard to hold down or he would vomit.

'Yes,' Nellie said. She squared her shoulders and suddenly her voice was strong. She stared at her big strong gardener's hands gripping the arms of her chair as she started to speak. 'You and Angus are twins,' she said.

'No!' Neil shouted. 'No!'

It was too much, intolerable. Why was she doing this, she was lying. He didn't need a brother, he and Nellie had each other. The two of them belonged together now, they had come to terms. There was no place for someone else. Neil felt bitterly resentful that she didn't even try to hide that he had never been enough for her, that she had thought about and searched for this stranger in spite of possessing

him. She should apologize, he thought, she has to say she's
sorry.

Nellie ignored Neil. It seemed to him that she had no
regard for his feelings as she said, 'I got pregnant when I
was fifteen. My parents didn't want anything to do with
me, so they turned me out. I didn't tell them. I kept it hidden
for as long as I could, and by then it was too late for an
abortion.'

Nellie hesitated, suddenly looking at Neil to gauge his
reaction to what she was saying. 'I don't know,' she said.
'If that's what you want to know, I don't know if I would
have had an abortion if I could. It was all so different then.
I couldn't get the money, I didn't have a choice.'

Nellie tried to run her fingers through her rough hair, but
they got caught up. She went on, her voice flat and, to him,
sounding hostile. 'I worked as a waitress for as long as I
could to save some money. There was an organization for
unmarried mothers and they helped me fix things up to have
the baby adopted. I was in a special home. We were supposed
to keep the babies until they were six weeks old. A doctor
I went to said he thought I'd got twins, and I was scared out
of my mind. I didn't say anything. I didn't know what to do.
I thought the adoption people would refuse to deal with two
babies; I even imagined the people at the home would
somehow manage to make sure only one survived being born.
It was probably just my imagination. I can't tell you . . .'

Her voice faltered and she gulped down the whisky left
in her glass.

She went on in that flat tone, like someone reading a list
of football results, 'I didn't say anything when I started
getting contractions. It was late on a Sunday and there was
only a skeleton staff on duty. No one was due that weekend.
Perhaps being twins brought it on early, I don't know. I'd
planned it all. I'd been keeping towels when I had a bath,
and I stole baby clothes from the other girls. So that night
when I knew it was all going to happen, I sneaked out very
early in the morning, about four o'clock, and went down
to the park and hid behind the bandstand. That's where you
and your brother were born.'

She stopped and took a deep breath, fighting to keep her voice from breaking down.

'He's not my brother,' Neil said. 'I don't have a brother. I won't.'

But Nellie ignored the interruption. She went on, 'I left one of the babies inside a bus shelter outside the railway station. It was a boy. I took you because you were crying and he wasn't, which would give me time to get away before anyone found him. I left ten pounds and some of the clothes pinned to the towel I wrapped him in. And I wrote a note saying his name was Angus and the doctor was wrong, there wasn't a twin and please, someone, look after him. Then I took you and caught a train to London and that was that.'

'What do you mean, that was that?' Neil said, his voice hard and cold. 'You can't leave it like that. How did you – we – end up in New Zealand?'

'I got a job as a waitress and Vince asked me out. He was on holiday in London – we got married and he took me home with him to New Zealand.'

She gave him a quick glance, then looked away. 'I did the best I could,' she said. 'He was a good dad to you, wasn't he?'

Neil shook his head, trying to take this in. He had loved his dad and now he felt that she had spoiled that for him too. She was trying to take something precious away from him. He was overwhelmed by dislike for her. He looked at her with icy objectivity, seeing the deep lines on her face, the worn skin, the tangled mop of grey hair she never bothered to brush, and he felt fear. He didn't know how to be alone. She had cast him off without a thought, and he was scared of what lay ahead. He was afraid that from now on he would hate her, want to hurt her, despise her.

He said, 'So who was my real father? What kind of a man does what he did, abandoning you when you were carrying his child?'

Nellie shrugged. 'God knows. Some lad I met at the local hop, I suppose. I liked a good time.'

Neil felt sick. He wanted to scream at her that she disgusted him, but he couldn't speak to her.

He couldn't take in that suddenly there was this brother,
let alone that that brother was Angus Dillon, of all people,
husband of pesky Joan. The irony was almost too much.
Neil suddenly wanted to laugh, but he knew he mustn't.

'What about Angus?' he asked then. He found it hard to
say the name.

'That's why I came back to England, to find Angus,' she
said. 'I must've been mad, I'd no way of tracing him. But
ever since I came back here, I've had this sort of conviction that one day I'd be in the street and I'd come face to
face with him, and we'd have found each other. It's silly,
isn't it? Whoever adopted him might have called him
anything. I didn't even know his name.'

'Now you do,' Neil said, 'you must be proud.'

It was brutal, but he had to lash out at her. He was
consumed with jealousy that she still thought about Angus,
she'd always thought about him. She'd got me, he thought,
why did she ever have to think of that long-lost other baby?

Nellie got up, and went to the mirror on the mantelpiece
above the fireplace to smear colour on her thin lips. The
lipstick had dried out from lack of use, and the colour caked
on her mouth.

'You look like a clown,' Neil said. 'No one will believe
you.'

'I've got to go to him,' she said. 'I've got to go down to
the police station and tell them he's my son and I want
to see him. He needs me.'

So do I, Ma, so do I, Neil felt he was screaming at her
but nothing he could say would change anything. He
came up behind her and the reflection of the two of them
stared back at him. He knew that he took after his mother,
he had always seen the likeness between them; but now
shock and fear had sharpened the outlines of his face, so
that the veneer of fat jollity had gone, leaving him haggard
and fearful.

My God, he thought, it could be Angus looking back at me.

'You see it now, don't you?' Nellie said, seeing his expression. She moved forward to touch his reflection in the glass.
'All the years apart, a different upbringing, a different life,

but it's there, isn't it? You're the mirror image of him. You're
Angus's twin brother. Oh, I've found my baby, it's a miracle.'

'Ma?' It was his cry for help. Neil thought he'd called
her aloud, but she took no notice and he wasn't sure he'd
spoken.

She turned away from the mirror to go through the
Victorian double doors and into the hall to get her coat.
She had put in these doors with their stained glass panels
as part of the improvements she'd made in the house. Not
only did they cut off any draughts through the hallway from
the front door, but she loved the way the light from the
sitting room cast patterns of jewelled light on the walls and
floor of the hall.

'Come on,' she said, 'aren't you pleased? I thought you'd
be happy . . .'

'No,' he said. 'No, no, no.' He closed the glass doors very
carefully, as though he were stopping himself from slamming
them. He said, 'I'm sorry, Ma, I can't explain, but you're *my*
mother, not his. I can't let you tell anyone he's your son.
There's nothing you can do for him, anyway. He's a middle-
aged man, he's nothing to do with you. He doesn't need a
mother now, he's got his own life. Just be glad you've found
him and leave it at that, please, I'm begging you.'

Nellie gave him a puzzled look. 'Are you jealous?' she
asked. 'Don't you want to have to share your poor old Ma?'
She was laughing at him, almost flirtatious, teasing him. 'I
did my best for you,' she said. 'I tried to love you. I tried
not to think of him. I called you Neil because it's so close
to Nellie, I thought it would bind us together. But it was
no good, it wasn't enough.'

She moved down the hall towards the front door.

Neil caught her arm and pulled her roughly back. 'You
can't do that,' he said. 'You can't tell the police anything.'

She was frightened at his tone and jerked away from him.

'For God's sake, Neil, he's your brother. My son. He
needs us.' The teasing tone had gone; she was getting angry.

'He's a child-killer,' Neil yelled at her, his face contorted
like a teenager throwing a tantrum. 'Your son's a child-
killer. You can't tell anyone about him.'

He jerked her arm back and pushed her aside so that she tripped and fell against the wall. He stepped past her and went out, slamming the front door behind him.

Then he turned the key of the deadlock from outside.

FOURTEEN

Sarah Makepeace and Jeff Acres had shared a house near the hospital in Hunsteignton for some time before they became what his colleagues on the newspaper called an item. The house was within walking distance of the Savill's office, and Sarah answered Jeff's advertisement for a housemate in the local paper. She liked his advert. She had become resistant to the lists of qualifications made by most of the would-be sharers, demands that only clinically hygienic, tidy, non-smoking, professional people without pets, or babies, or other idiosyncrasies should apply. Jeff had made no stipulations at all. And when she met him she liked him, too. He welcomed her because he liked her and they made each other laugh.

Much later, he told her how many chaotic, smoking, idio-syncratic pet-owning layabouts he'd rejected as sharers of his home, but by that time she took it as a joke and they were already lovers.

Sarah left Joan at the cottage after telling her about Angus's arrest. She wanted to be alone. She had to think what she should do next. She had expected Joan to take over the responsibility for protecting Angus against the police accu-sations. Joan was his wife, she was the one to defend him. Sarah was shocked at Joan's attitude, the way she seemed to be avoiding involvement. Joan of all people must know that Angus was innocent, that it was inconceivable that her husband could be a child-killer. If she doesn't know that, Sarah told herself bleakly, he hasn't a hope of persuading anyone else.

Her mind was in turmoil. It's none of my business, she told herself, I scarcely know Angus. But she knew she couldn't step back and wait for the police to acknowledge their mistake. She thought, I'm all he's got.

She got into her car and drove aimlessly, looking for

somewhere to stop. But whenever she saw a lay-by she
swept on regardless, driven to look for somewhere better.
As long as she kept on the move, she felt that she was
doing something to help. She didn't dare face up to the
huge fact that she was all that stood between Angus and
his conviction for a crime he didn't do. Poor Angus, she
thought, I'm not the knight in shining armour I'd choose if
I were in his shoes.

In spite of everything, though, in spite of Joan and the DNA
evidence and the certainty of those people in the village pub
that Angus was guilty, Sarah never wavered in her faith in
Angus's innocence.

Why? she asked herself, slowing down as she approached
yet another lay-by where she could stop to think. Why am
I so sure?

And the sound of the car tyres on the ribbed road surface,
as she spend towards a roundabout on to the motorway,
repeated a mocking refrain, 'You love him, you love him,
you love him.'

At the last moment she jerked the wheel and, instead of
taking the motorway access road, she carried on round the
roundabout and back the way she had come. The tyres
screamed in protest, and a car horn blared behind her. Oh,
God, she thought, I can't die yet, Angus needs me.

Back on the road to Hunsteignton, she began to drive
slowly and with almost excessive care. Her own notion
that she might be in love with Angus had come as a shock
to her. Am I in love with him? she asked herself, I can't
be. Why would I be? She was surprised at herself as she
thought, I wouldn't want to go on living in a world without
him. I don't care if he never loves me, I need him in my
life.

And then, as she found herself in the suburbs of
Hunsteignton and soon, too soon, on her own street, she
found herself inexplicably filled with an extraordinary
happiness.

Jeff was at home when she let herself into the house. For
a moment, she wondered who this stranger was, and then
she wished she hadn't come home because she didn't want

to be brought down to earth by finding the practicalities of her life unchanged.

'You're home,' she said. It was a feeble thing to say. She was startled at the sound of her own voice, it seemed to her to reflect her new uninterest in the way things were with Jeff. Surely he could tell that something had changed, that she was no longer the same person he'd kissed goodbye that morning?

'Where've you been?' he said, and she could hear he was accusing her. So he can tell, she thought, he knows something's up, he's going to make a fuss.

'I had to see someone in Otterbrook,' she said. She made a conscious effort to keep her voice light. She didn't want to have to deal with anything to do with Jeff or her life before today.

'Who was that, then?' he asked.

Does he always interrogate me like this? she asked herself. He sounds as though he thinks he owns me.

'*Her* name's Joan Dillon, if you must know,' Sarah said.

'Joan Dillon?' he said, surprised. 'The woman married to the man they've taken in for the Tara Davidson killing? How do you know her?'

Damn, Sarah thought, he won't drop it now. He's like a sniffer dog scenting blood. She bit her lip. She must try to think clearly. It had been stupid of her to mention Joan like that. Of course Jeff would be covering Angus's case, he was the senior reporter on the paper.

He brought her a glass of wine.

He's preparing to interview me, she told herself.

'You look as though you could do with this,' he said.

She looked into his brown eyes, which always seemed to her full of humour and tolerance at human failing. His eyes and his smile were what had first made her so sure she could trust him, whatever happened.

'Have the police really got a watertight case against Angus?' she asked.

'I suppose they'll have to check out alibis and witnesses and so on, but one of the cops on the case told me today that there's a DNA match,' Angus said.

Sarah recoiled slightly at the satisfaction in his tone. She'd
heard it before when he'd nailed a good story and beaten
the opposition to it.

'But what sort of DNA evidence are they talking about?
Surely it could be chance, if it was taken from . . . well,
from something like a cigarette or a hair at the scene of
crime? To be sure, surely they'd need semen or something,
wouldn't they? Or signs of her blood on his clothes, something like that?'

Jeff laughed. 'I don't think there's much chance of that,
not after the delay before the body was found.'

'Well, semen, then. Wasn't the girl working as a prostitute? He could've been a client. It wouldn't necessarily
mean he'd killed her, would it?'

'Hey,' Jeff said, laughing at her, 'what's with all the questions? Is Dillon's wife going to defend him and enlisted
you to pump me for details of the police evidence?'

'No,' Sarah said, and then she blurted out, 'she's not
interested. She's taken up with someone else, and she thinks
the police will realize they've made a mistake. If he isn't
guilty, that is.'

Sarah saw the look on Jeff's face as she said that, and
she could have bitten out her tongue. She hadn't meant to
get carried away by her resentment at Joan's attitude. She
tried to backtrack, but she knew it was too late; she could
see the gleam in Jeff's eyes, which she'd seen too often
before when he got the scent of a good story.

He said, and she knew he was trying to keep any excitement out of his voice, 'A mistake, eh? Does she think that?
Why should she think that?'

'Oh, drop it, Jeff. I don't want to talk about her.'

'No, but why? Why should she think the police would
make a mistake like that?'

Sarah shouted at him, 'Because it happened before, that's
why.'

And then she was lost; he pressed her into telling him
about that day on the common looking for poor Julie.

'They questioned Angus because his DNA was on a
cigarette butt by her body,' she said. 'But he got through most

of a packet while he was waiting at the scene for me to get
the police, of course there were fag ends with his DNA on.'

Jeff sounded gleeful. 'So now they'll reopen the
Makepeace case and they can tie him in to that?' he said.
'It's a fantastic story. The nationals won't even have a sniff
of it yet.'

'You can't use it as a story,' Sarah said, aghast. 'I was
there. It wasn't true, he didn't kill Julie. She was my niece,
for God's sake. If you publish anything about what I told
you, I'll never forgive you.'

'Sarah, the man's a paedophile. He's going down for
killing a young girl and now it seems he probably killed a
kid years ago. A kid you were related to, how can you be
like this? Surely you can't defend him?'

'I know he didn't do it,' she said. She was angry now. 'I'm
sure you and your sleazy colleagues can make it look as
though he must be guilty by association, but I happen to
believe he's innocent until he's proved guilty, and all you've
got is coincidence. I know he didn't kill Julie, and I don't
believe he killed this other girl, whatever the police say. And
if you try to quote me on any of this, I'll deny it.'

'Hey,' Jeff said, not sure if she was serious, 'what is this?
How come you're getting yourself so het up?'

Sarah said, 'It makes me sick the way you and everyone
else takes it for granted he's guilty when you don't know
anything about him.'

Jeff was offended. He prided himself on being a dis-
passionate and objective judge simply by virtue of being a
reporter. He disliked particularly the way Sarah included
him with everyone else.

'I know quite a lot about your friend Angus Dillon,
actually,' he said.

Sarah resented his smug tone, as though there could be
no argument about his superior knowledge.

He went on, 'I don't like to spoil your persecution fantasy
about him, but it's my job to report the facts. What you
told me about Dillon's DNA matching samples found with
Julie's body is a fact and it's part of the story. So's the fact
that his wife's leaving him.'

'None of which has anything to do with the police case against Angus now,' she insisted.

'You'll have to let me be the judge of that,' said Jeff, with all the patronizing superiority of a man who feels he is representing the public interest.

Sarah forced herself not to react. If she lost her temper with him, she might say something she would regret. The last thing Angus needed was for her to alienate Jeff and give him cause to be vindictive.

'OK,' she said, 'let's drop it.'

'I wish it was that easy,' Jeff said. 'It's not my job to prove the case against the man, but you must see that if the cases are connected I can't ignore it.'

'I guess not,' she said, unable to keep the bitterness out of her voice, 'but if it's so important to you that you'd use me to stand it up, even though I've told you it's not true, then, as far as I'm concerned, that's the end of us.'

There was a pause. She glared at Jeff, and he tried to stare her down, but she held his gaze until at last he dropped his eyes.

'I'll leave you out of it, if it means that much to you,' he said. 'But on one condition. I want us to get married. Soon. What do you say?'

Curiously, Sarah was not surprised at this sudden proposal. Or that he should resort to blackmail. For some time, she had expected Jeff to ask her to marry him. And, for most of that time, she had put off admitting to herself that she wasn't sure about it. She had tried to avoid any opportunities for him to introduce the subject because she did not know how she wanted to answer.

But now, when it came to it, she knew that she had no intention of accepting him. She was happy enough living with him, she enjoyed sharing the house with him, she liked him. A week ago – yesterday, even – she might even have said yes. Today, she knew that the only man she ever wanted to marry was Angus. It had suddenly hit her. She loved Angus. It was her fault, though, if Jeff took her agreement to marry him for granted. She had never given him any reason to doubt it. Indeed, she never had doubted it; she'd expected herself that they would marry one day, simply not yet.

I can't say no, she thought, because if I do he's got a right to know why, and if he even imagines it could be because of Angus, he could make things much worse for him. People believe what they read in the papers.

'Ask me again when you're not trying to bribe me,' she said, and laughed so that he'd know she was making fun.

He hugged her. She knew that he thought she was saying yes, because it had never occurred to him that she wouldn't.

Oh, God, she thought, what am I doing? What am I going to do?

FIFTEEN

Nellie took several minutes to recover her breath after Neil had gone. She was shocked that her son had pushed her so roughly.

There was a small settle against the wall in the hall, and she sat there until the beating of her heart no longer filled her ears and she didn't have to pant for breath.

She said aloud, 'What's got into him? What's the matter?'

Then she got up and walked slowly back to the stained glass doors. She thought she would rest for a while in the sitting room, giving Neil a chance to calm down. At any moment, she expected that he would be back with that funny lopsided grin on his face he'd had as a little boy when he knew he'd done something wrong and wanted her to forgive him.

She turned the door handle. Nothing happened. The doors were locked.

Nellie turned the brass handles one way, then the other. Still nothing happened. She shook them and tried again. Then she knelt down and examined the lock. There was no doubt about the solid bar firmly in place in the keep. And when she peered through the keyhole to see if the key was in place on the inside of the door, she could see light the other side. It wasn't some freak accident then; he had deliberately locked the doors and taken the key.

Nellie got slowly to her feet and walked back across the shimmering rich reds and greens and blues of the reflected stained glass bouncing off the tiled floor of the hallway. She tried the front door. Neil had turned the deadlock. There was nothing she could do to open it.

She returned to sit on the settle. She remembered her much younger self sitting stiff and upright like this outside the head teacher's office, waiting to be punished for something. She felt like that now. Perhaps it was a mistake? Neil hadn't been thinking straight, he was upset, perhaps he'd locked the door automatically because he was in a hurry to get out of the house.

What am I going to do? Nellie asked herself. He may not be back for hours. I'm trapped.

She wished now that she hadn't moved the telephone into the sitting room. She'd done that because it was so much warmer in there, and in the winter the wind positively howled around the hallway.

Then she considered breaking the stained glass, but she couldn't bear to carry out such an act of vandalism. She loved those original Victorian panes. Anyway, she told herself, I couldn't lean through and open the door because there's no key. Even if I broke the glass in both panels I don't think I'd have room to crawl through.

It was pointless to shout, either, or bang on the door. The road was some distance away from the house, and it wasn't the sort of place anyone ever walked. And Nellie's nearest neighbour was nearly quarter of a mile away.

Neil is such a silly boy, she told herself. He's doing this because he didn't want me to go dashing off to the police to tell them about Angus. He's jealous, she told herself, he likes having me to himself. Then she thought, I should have been more sensitive. I should've realized how upset he'd be to find out like that he'd got a brother after being an only child for so long. Of course he needs time to adjust. He'll be back as soon as he's sorted himself out a bit. I've only got to wait.

Gradually the colours through the stained glass dimmed and the light faded in the hall. Nellie sat for some time in the dark. She felt as though she was in a curious state of suspension, as though time had stopped and was sitting beside her on the settle waiting for Neil to come home.

Slowly she began to wonder if Neil would return that night. Has he left me as some sort of punishment because I left my baby? she asked herself. But why should he? He wasn't the one I abandoned, it was Angus.

And then she thought, he's jealous, he won't share. If he can't have me to himself, he doesn't want anything to do with me. My God, is he going to leave me here to die?

She tried to pull herself together. Don't be so silly, she told herself, Neil's my son, he loves me, he'd never do anything like that.

She was trembling. It was very cold. But it wasn't the cold that made her tremble; it was fear.

It might have been hours later, or perhaps much less, when she heard a key in the front door. Then she had to screw up her eyes as Neil turned on the lights.

He seemed surprised to see her sitting in the hall. You fool, she said to herself, look at the state you got yourself into without any reason at all. She was ashamed, and guilty that she could have thought that this cheerful, loving son of hers could be the monster of her morbid imagination.

'What are you doing sitting here in the dark, Ma?' Neil said. 'Why didn't you turn on the lights?'

Nellie was confused. 'I don't know,' she said, 'I didn't think of it.'

Neil laughed. 'You fell asleep sitting there, didn't you, and you don't want to admit it? What are you doing in the hall, anyway? That settle's horribly uncomfortable.'

'The doors are locked,' she said, 'I couldn't go into the sitting room.'

'Locked? Don't be silly, how would the doors be locked?'

Neil walked past her to check the doors. He fiddled for a moment, then the doors opened. 'There,' he said, 'they weren't locked. You have to lift one side a bit, then the catch works. How could they be locked, there isn't even a key?'

He was standing there smiling at her and she didn't know what to think. How could she make a mistake like that? She'd been so sure that those doors were locked, but when he showed her the knack of lifting as she turned the knob, it was so simple. Seeing Angus on the television had been too much of a shock, it had thrown her totally off beam.

They were locked, she told herself, why would I make a mistake like that?

'I'm getting old,' she said, 'I suppose I panicked.'

'You go and sit down and I'll make us a quick omelette. You'll be better with something inside you. You shouldn't blame yourself, you couldn't open the door and you panicked, that's all.'

'Oh God,' she said, 'what about Angus? I should go to him.'

'Too late today,' Neil said, bringing her a glass of sherry. 'You sit down and drink that and we'll talk about it over supper. There's no point going down to see the cops tonight, though, you'll only get half-witted youngsters on the night shift to talk to. You need to tell a senior officer about this. We'll go there first thing in the morning. I'll come with you.'

Nellie looked up at his familiar friendly face beaming down at her. He was worried about her, she could see a little frown of concern even as he smiled at her.

'Yes,' she said, 'you're right. I'm such a silly old thing. You've no idea what I was imagining while I was sitting there waiting for you to come home.'

'Well, for now, you can let me do the worrying,' Neil said. 'Do you want to watch television while I'm cooking? *Pretty Woman*'s on again. You always like that.'

'Thanks, son,' Nellie said.

Neil took her glass and refilled it, then disappeared into the kitchen to cook. She heard the clash of pans as he got to work.

She was unconscious by the time Neil came back into the room to check.

He turned off the television. For a while he stood watching her.

He took Nellie's empty glass and sniffed the dregs of the sherry. Then he nodded with satisfaction.

'You'll feel much better after a good night's sleep, Ma,' he said.

He pulled her up out of the chair. She was heavier than he'd expected, but he managed to hoist her over his shoulder. It reminded him of times he'd almost forgotten now; when his stepfather had passed out drunk in the living room and Neil had had to take Vince upstairs to bed. Vince had gone on a lot of benders after Nellie left the two of them in New Zealand and went back to England. Neil remembered that only too well. He'd never blamed Vince; the poor man had been devastated at losing Nellie.

No, Neil always knew it was his mother's fault, for leaving Vince and for leaving him. And for no reason that either of them could understand.

He carried his mother upstairs to her bedroom and dumped her on the bed.

He looked down at her as she lay on the cover, her breathing harsh. Well, now I know, he thought, you came here to look for him. You turned your back on me and Vince, who'd always loved you, to look for someone who's got every reason to hate you.

For some time he hesitated; then, slowly and carefully, he set about undressing her. His mouth twisted with distaste as he pulled off her shoes to reveal her gnarled feet, then her baggy jeans. He was appalled by the dry scaly feel of her skin and the hideous yellowish folds of her belly under her dull black pants. He did not try to remove them, almost gagging at the thought of what they covered.

He thought, it's revolting, this hideous process of decay. This loathsome old body gave birth to me, this old woman is my mother. And then he told himself, there must be a God. There can be nothing random about such perfect cynical revenge against the human parasites He created in His image. Hatred like that frightened Neil, but he admired it nonetheless. He thought, that takes genius, but then, as a finishing touch, He outlawed killing the creatures He'd created to cleanse the earth.

Neil smiled, addressing God, 'Never had the courage of your convictions, did you, you old tyrant?' he mocked.

Then he spoke to the unconscious Nellie. 'If it's hatred you want, you bitch,' he said, 'you've got it now.'

Nellie groaned, moved, and started to snore. Neil had to escape. He pulled the bedclothes roughly up to cover her body and turned to go.

'Payback time, Ma,' he said as he went out, closing and locking the door behind him.

SIXTEEN

'We've got to talk to the wife. What's holding things up there?'

Detective Chief Inspector Gifford was in a bad mood. He knew he should be feeling pleased with himself. He'd got an open and shut case against a child-killer, enough evidence to satisfy the Crown Prosecution Service anyway; and on top of that there was a chance he could clear up several similar cases in the past once the killer realized his case was hopeless and there was no point in not confessing. Angus Dillon had been a journalist, he knew the score; he'd know he hadn't a cat in hell's chance of ever getting out of jail on this one. He might as well come clean. At least the families of his victims could find some sort of closure.

And yet Charlie Gifford was not happy: something in the back of his mind about this case nagged at him like toothache.

'It's too damned easy,' he grumbled to Sergeant Knowles, who nodded and muttered, and hoped something else would come up to take the boss's mind off his stupid and irrational doubts. That was the trouble with an old-fashioned detective like Charlie Gifford; he could never resist going the extra mile. Over the years, in Knowles's view, the boss had destroyed a lot of sure-fire convictions this way. Gifford called his reservations a hunch; Knowles thought it was more like the sort of airy-fairy shenanigans old women with scarves round their heads tried with tea leaves.

Knowles answered his boss's original question. 'We've called and left messages for the Dillon woman,' he said, 'but she wasn't at work and she doesn't seem to be home much at the moment. Apparently, she spent at least one night at a rather sleazy motel off the A30, but we haven't had much luck pinning her down.'

Sergeant Knowles decided not to mention that no one had really tried very hard to get hold of Joan Dillon. It had seemed like an irrelevance to Knowles, with the evidence they had against her husband. There was always the chance that she would lie and give him an alibi, so it was best not to ask. But with the Chief Inspector in his present mood, he thought he should say as little as possible.

'Well, come on then, what are you waiting for?' Inspector Gifford said. 'If she's not at work maybe she's at the cottage now. There's nowhere else for her to go. She's a solicitor, isn't she? I expect her colleagues will be glad enough for her to stay away from the office. It can't be a good advertisement for a firm of lawyers, employing the wife of a man charged with killing a kid. She's bound to be trying to distance herself from our inquiries.'

'Very embarrassing, I should think,' Knowles said. 'Specially as the kid was on the game and hubby may well have been one of a child prostitute's clients.'

As Knowles drove out of Hunsteignton towards Otterbrook, Gifford sat in the passenger seat scowling at the passing countryside. It was one of those bleak days when everything looks grey and half-dead in an east wind, but the Chief Inspector did not even notice.

'There's something that bothers me, Joe,' he said at last, 'I've tried to tell myself it's not important but it bothers me.'

'What's that, sir?'

Knowles, who disliked driving in the narrow lanes as they left the town behind, didn't sound very interested.

'Why didn't he have sex with them? The man's a pervert who gets off on abducting young girls, but there's no sign at all of sexual interference. So why does he do it? What's he after?'

'There were signs of semen on the handkerchief,' Knowles said. 'Isn't that what our DNA evidence is based on?'

'The handkerchief found at the scene of crime with Dillon's DNA on it? Yes, that's true. But no sign on the body. Not on Julie Makepeace's either.'

'Well, that was a long time ago in forensic terms,' Knowles said. 'We can't rule it out.'

Gifford was still thinking about what his Sergeant had said when Knowles banged on the front door of the cottage and, after some delay, Joan Dillon answered it.

Gifford was startled at the sight of her. What did I expect? he asked himself. Did I want sackcloth and ashes? He thought, she doesn't look embarrassed in the least, she looks bloody radiant, as though she hasn't a care in the world, and I don't like it.

'Mrs Dillon?' he asked. 'Mrs Angus Dillon?'

'Joan Dillon,' she said, 'Ms Joan Dillon.' She smiled to show she wasn't being unfriendly, simply reminding him that they lived in post-feminist times. 'Are you from the police? You've taken your time. I've been expecting you.'

Sergeant Knowles pretended he didn't notice the hard look the Chief Inspector gave him when she said that. He was in for a bollocking later for his little white lie about not being able to pin Joan Dillon down.

'Some sort of administrative mistake at a lower level, I'm afraid,' he said.

'We'd like to ask you a few questions,' Gifford said.

'You'd better come in,' she said.

She led them through to the sitting room, which reminded Gifford of an old-fashioned saloon bar in a country pub.

'Sit down, won't you?' she said. 'I'm afraid I don't think I'll be able to help you very much. Angus and I haven't really been close for some time now.'

'He says that you can confirm he was at home here on the night that Tara Davidson disappeared, and then all weekend until she was found. Is that so?'

'Oh, is that right?' Joan said. She made a pretence of trying to remember, which fooled neither of the policemen, and then asked: 'Exactly when was it we're talking about?'

'Saturday the tenth,' Knowles said.

Joan flushed. She could feel that these men disliked her, and she knew why. It's because they think Angus is scum, they take it for granted I'm like him, she thought, and she felt angry with Angus that he had laid her open to their hostility.

'No, you see, I can't help you,' she said. 'I wasn't here

that weekend. So I can't confirm anything. Not that that helps you much, I'm afraid, because if I can't confirm Angus's alibi, I can't say it wasn't true, either.'

She smiled as though she thought she had said something clever. Inspector Gifford sighed as though he had heard it all before.

'May I ask where you were, Ms Dillon?' he said.

'I was with a friend,' Joan said.

'What was the name of your friend, please?'

'I don't have to tell you that,' she said angrily. 'I'm not suspected of anything, am I?'

'This is a murder inquiry,' Sergeant Knowles said. 'We have to ask these questions. The name?'

Joan hesitated as though she would refuse, then shrugged. 'I don't see the relevance of your questions,' she said, 'but if you want to know, his name is Neil Carver.'

'Address?'

Joan visualized these heavy-handed cops barging in on Neil's old mother with their clumsy questions about the husband of a girlfriend of Neil's she had never heard about. No, better keep them away from the dreaded mother.

'He's an architect. He works at Savill's in the High Street. I can't help you with more than that. We go to hotels, or he comes here.' She was lying out of bravado.

'Here? Were you here with him the weekend in question?'

Oh, my God, she thought, they'll find out we went to his house when his mother was away.

'No,' she said coldly. 'We went out and I got back very late.'

'We'll catch up with Mr Carver at Savill's if we have to,' Inspector Gifford said.

'Yes,' Joan said, 'you do that.'

She moved towards the door as though she expected them to be on their way. But neither of the policemen moved.

'Would you say you were happily married, Ms Dillon?' Gifford asked.

'What has this got to do with anything?' Joan snapped at him.

'Sex life all right?' Knowles asked.

'Get out of my house,' Joan said to Gifford, ignoring Knowles.

'We're trying to establish why Mr Dillon would be in the red light district of Hunsteignton picking up a child prostitute,' Inspector Gifford said gently. There was a wheedling note in his voice as he went on, 'You see, on the face of it that would seem to be out of character, but maybe it wasn't? These are serious charges against him, and we have to be very careful about getting the facts right.'

Knowles was irritated that his boss seemed to be pleading with a child-killer's wife. She must've had some idea what was going on, women always did.

'Did he know you were playing away?' he demanded rudely.

'I've already tried to tell you, my husband and I have lived separate lives for years. If you have to ask intrusive questions, I wish you'd listen to the answers. Now I'd like you to leave.'

Gifford said, 'Please, Ms Dillon, can you think of anything you could tell us that might help us to pin down what your husband was doing that weekend? I mean, did you ring him? Or did he ring you about anything at all? Any little thing might help.'

Joan turned away and went back into the room to sit down. Gifford's questions had reminded her, she did ring Angus that Saturday night. She'd rung on her mobile while Neil was in the bathroom. She'd thought Angus would be out and she could leave a message saying she had to go out of town to see a client. She was embarrassed when Angus, sounding half-asleep, answered in person. She'd put the phone down quickly.

He had been at the cottage, then. But Joan hesitated. She didn't want to have to explain to these offensive cops.

I don't want to be involved, she thought, I don't want to be dragged into this. It's bad enough if they quiz Neil about whether I was with him, but at least when he says I was, that'll be the end of it. If I say anything about ringing

Angus, I'll never hear the end of it. I don't want anything to do with it.

And then she told herself, if I answer their stupid questions, I'm validating their case against Angus. They haven't got a case, because what they imagine is impossible. We've been here before. They've got some glitch in their system which they should've put right after the last time, but they didn't. Maybe they will this time. We'll sue for compensation, make them pay. That might make them do something about it.

'I can't remember,' she said. 'Why don't you check the phone records? Someone else may have called and talked to him. You could confirm Angus's alibi with that, couldn't you?'

'We have that in hand, Madam,' Knowles said.

'Madam', Joan thought, mocking him. Policeman or no policeman, the man's a twerp. He was born to be a flunkey. Madam, indeed!

SEVENTEEN

S arah put down the phone when Jeff came into the sitting room.

Something in the mulish set of her jaw caught his attention. He noticed, too, that her knuckles were white where she had been gripping the receiver for some time.

'You're home early,' she said, and there was still an edge of exasperated tension in her voice that Jeff recognized from bitter experience. She had been tackling officialdom.

'Just came home to change,' he said. 'I'm covering the Chamber of Commerce dinner tonight.'

'Oh,' Sarah said. She had scarcely heard what he said.

'Who were you ringing?' he asked.

Sarah stifled the urge to tell him to mind his own business. Frustrated by bureaucrats, it would be a relief to pick a fight with him. But there was no point in making things worse.

She said, 'I've been trying to get through to book a visit to Angus for nearly an hour,' she said. 'And then when I do get through, they say I don't have to book, he hasn't been there fourteen days yet so I can have a reception visit tomorrow.'

'You're going to visit Angus Dillon?' he said.

'Yes.' Sarah was defiant. 'I said I'm his sister, so they didn't ask questions.'

'Good girl,' he said, 'glad you're on the case. We'll make a great team.'

My God, Sarah thought, did I ever really seriously consider marrying this man?

'They'll want ID,' Jeff said.

'I know, they said. A photo driving licence will do. That's all right. I could be his married sister. Or his half-sister.'

'What time are you going tomorrow?' Jeff asked.

'Afternoon. After one thirty p.m.'

'I'll jot down a few questions we need him to answer. You can take them with you,' Jeff said.

Sarah had the piece of paper he'd given her in her pocket when she arrived at the frowning grey prison building on the outskirts of Hunsteignton the next day. Jeff had handed it to her as he left for work and she'd folded it away without looking at it. Now, expecting that she would be searched, she took it out and tore it into scraps.

As she approached the entrance, she had the uncomfortable feeling that she was being watched. She looked for a litter bin, feeling an unseeing eye waiting to pounce if she dropped the scraps of paper, expecting a snatch squad to descend and arrest her on suspicion of conspiracy.

There was a litter bin at the gate. She got rid of the scraps of paper and felt relieved, her innocence restored.

She waited at a plastic-topped table in a visitor centre which reminded her of the setting for school exams. She felt now the same gnawing fear in her stomach as she'd had then. She thought, these days they probably search the kids in school the same way they did me here, looking for knives. Putting her bag and keys and things in a locker had been like school, too. But at school she'd never had the feeling that the staff, once she'd mentioned Angus's name, wouldn't really have cared if she'd sneaked in a lethal weapon and used it on him. She shivered at a sudden inkling of the terror a real paedophile faced, not just in this place, but in the world at large.

Angus was suddenly sitting facing her across the table.

'My favourite sister,' he said, 'you'll never know how glad I am to see you.' He smiled, and she found it hard to fight back tears.

He was looking tired, and his prison-issue clothes hung on him, as though he'd been given garments several sizes too big as an added humiliation due to the nature of his crime. But there was still a wry twinkle in his eye as he looked at Sarah. He still isn't taking this seriously, she thought.

'Are they treating you all right?' she asked. She thought, well, what else can I ask? They're probably recording every word we say to use in evidence against him.

'I thought Joan would have confirmed my alibi and I'd be out by now,' he said.

'I don't know,' she said. 'They seem to think they've a DNA match. My housemate is a reporter and that's what he said.'

'This is worse than last time, isn't it?' Angus said. He sounded matter of fact, not intimidated by the monstrous unfairness of what was happening to him.

'Angus, you've got to think,' she said. 'How can your DNA be on that girl's body?'

'Was it on her body?' he asked. 'Or on something at the scene, like it was with the cigarette stub with Julie?'

Sarah shook her head. 'I don't know. Does it make any difference?'

'Well, yes, I think so,' Angus said slowly. 'If it was something at the scene, and that poor girl was found on the common, maybe I have been there. I walk on the common a lot. I could've stopped to blow my nose and dropped a tissue, or torn something I was wearing and left a scrap of cloth. I could've eaten an apple and thrown away the core, or something could've fallen out of my pocket . . .'

'And if it was on the body?' Sarah prompted him.

'Then somebody is setting me up,' Angus said.

He was watching her for her reaction.

It's true, Sarah told herself, it has to be true. The DNA has to be his, the police wouldn't be making a mistake like that. Someone hates Angus and they're setting him up.

She thought of the people she'd overheard at that horrible pub in Otterbrook. One of them could be a pervert who'd picked on Angus as a fall guy to be blamed for his own crimes. Or hers. It could be a woman. All those people must know about what happened after Julie was found, he'd be an obvious sucker for the real criminal.

'Who? Who's doing it? It must be someone you know.'

Sarah knew she sounded brutal, but there was no point in pussyfooting round the fact that someone Angus knew could do this.

'I don't know.' Angus lifted his fingers where they were gripping the edge of the table in a gesture of helplessness. 'I've thought and thought, and I don't know.'

Sarah suddenly thought of Jeff. Early on, as the local reporter, Jeff would have had access to the crime scene when the body was found. He'd got good friends among the local cops.

She asked herself, could Jeff be jealous? He could've suspected that he was losing me before I told him. He could've spied on me. But what would he have against Angus? He doesn't know Angus, he couldn't have plotted anything like this.

'You thought of someone?' Angus asked. 'I saw it in your face.'

Sarah felt ashamed that she could even have imagined that Jeff could do anything like this.

'No,' she said, 'I suddenly thought that my boyfriend might be jealous of you, but it's ridiculous. He'd never do anything so monstrous.'

'Your boyfriend the housemate?' Angus said, and grinned at her as though they were having this conversation somewhere completely different, over dinner, or on a picnic, somewhere far from this grim room under the eyes of people who hated them for what they thought Angus had done.

'Is it ridiculous that this boyfriend might be jealous of me?' he asked.

'No,' Sarah said, 'but we can't talk about that now. We've got to put a stop to this nightmare first. Who'd have access to something with your DNA on it?'

'Well, lots of people, if it's things I use in an everyday way. If we're talking intimate samples, of course, that's different.'

'Joan?'

'Joan and I are far from intimate, but I suppose so.'

'Neil? Isn't he her boyfriend? Maybe he thinks she still loves you?'

'No, he wouldn't think that. And anyway, why? I'm not standing in his way. I've wished them joy of each other. I suspect he's not as keen as she is, and if so, isn't it more in his interest to keep me on the scene?'

Sarah said, 'The Neil I know avoids commitment like the plague. He wouldn't want you out of the way.'

She saw Angus's expression and knew he still cared about Joan. She wished she hadn't said anything. 'I don't know what to do,' she said.

'Maybe your jealous friend could tell you what the DNA evidence is? If he doesn't know he could find out if he's any kind of a reporter,' Angus said. He seemed more animated than he had when he'd first sat down at the table. 'Do you think you could get it out of him?'

'I'll have a go,' she said. 'And you try to think of anyone who might hold a grudge against you. Or Joan, even.'

A siren sounded to call the end of the visit. Angus got up to go. He kissed Sarah briefly. 'A sisterly embrace,' he said, 'I don't want anyone to think I'm some kind of pervert.'

'I'm not giving up on you,' Sarah said. 'If you have got a secret enemy, I promise he's going to have a fight on his hands, whoever it is.'

EIGHTEEN

Neil put a tray with a jug of water and a glass on Nellie's bedside table.

'Wake up, sleepyhead,' he said, pouring water into the glass, 'time for your pills.'

Nellie opened her eyes and stared at him, confused. Through the window, which faced west into the prevailing wind, the sun was low in the sky, filling the room with red light. There was the sound of heavy rush hour traffic from the road.

'Neil? What's happening? What time is it?'

She struggled to sit up in the bed, but she seemed strangely weak, scarcely able to move.

'Don't you worry about anything,' Neil said. 'Are you feeling any better?'

'Why am I in bed at this time of day?' she demanded, but it sounded querulous in the feeble voice which was all she could muster.

'You had a bit of a turn, Ma,' Neil said, sounding deliberately cheery as he handed her pills and then the glass of water. 'The doctor's been and says there's nothing to worry about, but you're to stay where you are and rest. No getting up or getting upset for a few days.'

'Which doctor came? I don't remember any doctor,' Nellie said. 'How did I get here? Who undressed me?'

'Dr Smith came,' Neil said. 'He's the locum. Now, take these and go back to sleep. You'll soon be feeling better. But no more questions now. Here, this pill, too.'

Nellie swallowed the last of the pills and Neil took the empty glass from her and put it down beside the jug. His mother put her mole-like hands to her head as though checking to see it was still there. 'I feel ever so queer,' she said. 'Are you all right coping, son? I'll come down a bit later and cook us something to eat.'

'You lie there and rest, Ma. And straight to sleep. Dr Smith said you needed plenty of sleep.' Neil added, under his breath, 'And you're going to get it.'

Nellie slumped against the pillows, scarcely conscious. She was muttering to herself, but Neil wasn't interested in listening to her.

'Sleep tight, Ma,' he said. He closed the door and then locked it behind him.

He took his mother's old pickup and drove into Hunsteignton, and then across the town centre and through the inner suburbs to the Walker council estate beyond. He wouldn't risk taking his own car into an area like this, it would be asking for trouble.

The Walker Estate was a blot on the fair face of Hunsteignton. Everyone said so. The residents were all criminals and anyone who went there was liable to get mugged, or knifed, or simply beaten up as a way of passing the day. From time to time the Borough Council debated what could be done about the crime and vandalism there, but nothing came of their discussions. There was no political will to act. No one saw any advantage in fighting a lost cause; and many tacitly agreed that it was better to contain the problems within the Walker Estate rather than risk dispersing them into less volatile districts. The police and the fire service had given up going into the Walker except in emergency, and ambulances were often called but found it hard to penetrate hostile gangs of youths. Even social workers tended to put aside their case files about families there, piling them back into their pending trays until the papers slipped to the floor and could be legitimately binned. So the vulnerable lived in terror of the hordes of feral teenagers marauding the streets on the hunt for whatever they could find to pass the time.

Neil loved this place. The threat of danger lurking round every street corner, in every grim building, excited him. Time and again it drew him back to drive slowly through the hopeless streets. He relished the devastation, the burned out carcasses of cars, the barricaded broken windows, the few poverty-stamped shops trading behind metal grilles.

The groups of drugged and drunken kids moving en masse, like prowling rats among the squalid concrete buildings, fascinated him as he drove past them. Sometimes the gangs would try to stop the car, throwing themselves against the closed windows and beating out a macabre anthem on the metal with staves or chains. Neil laughed at them, high on the raw danger. Somehow they seemed to sense his exhilaration and were disconcerted. They fed on fear, not excitement.

But he never stopped.

One day I will, he told himself, one day I'll find out what happens next.

But he never would. He had another dangerous game to play.

That night he did not have to wait long for what he wanted. He parked on the outskirts of the estate, where the late-night buses stopped and turned back into town. Between buses, once any passengers had hurried off, the street was dark and deserted like an abandoned film set.

Then came a young girl on her own, finding her way home. A young girl taking her first steps towards being grown-up, dressed like a caricature of celebrity chic. A girl too young to drink, who'd gone out to a club with older girls and drunk far too much. In the crush she'd lost touch with anyone she knew, lost all her inhibitions in the intoxicating caress of alcohol and strangers' bodies against her own.

Her skirt scarcely covered her sex. Her nipples tried to thrust through the thin material of her skimpy top. She looked ridiculous, like a badly operated puppet in her high heels and naked rubber legs. But Neil could feel the heat off her as he stopped the car beside her and wound down the window.

'I'm looking for Medway Street,' he said. 'Can you tell me how to get there?'

She staggered towards the sound of his voice. She was hopelessly, helplessly drunk.

'Hey,' he said gently, 'don't cry. Did your friends leave you behind, and you had to walk home alone?' His voice was soft, like a caress. 'Do your parents know you're out this late?'

She stood, swaying a little, staring at him.

He said in his soft voice, as though he were soothing a frightened animal, 'Don't be scared. I've got a daughter your age, I know what happens. You're safe now. I'll look after you.'

'They were supposed to wait for me,' she managed to say, 'I told them I'd be back.'

'You went off with a boy, didn't you? Just for a little while?'

He watched her as she tried to gather her wits. 'He dumped me,' she wailed, 'and everyone had gone.'

'Come on,' he said, 'you can't stay out here all night. Get in, I'll look after you.'

She felt her way round the car to get in the passenger seat. As she sat back, she puffed out her cheeks and blew out the air in a childish gesture, which made her sound like an old woman glad to get the weight off her feet. She was scarcely conscious, making no attempt to pull her skirt down over her thin, splayed thighs. Neil gave thanks to whatever spotty youth had brought her to such a pitch of sexual hunger. When he leaned over to close the passenger door, his arm brushed against her breasts and she grabbed his hand and placed it inside her top against her naked nipple.

'Please,' she muttered, eyes closed.

He bent his head and touched the tip of her breast with his tongue. She moaned, and her child's hands took his head and tried to pull his mouth closer.

Dirty little bitch, he thought, even if this is the first time.

'Not here,' he murmured, 'I know where we can go.'

He drove towards Studleigh Common. It was very late and he met no traffic on the way. The girl, passed out now, lay slumped in the seat. From time to time he stroked the top of her narrow thigh with his left hand, slipping his finger between the hot, swollen lips of her clitoris, and without waking she opened her legs wider and he could feel her wet flesh sucking him in.

This is stupid, Neil kept telling himself, it's madness.

And then he thought, no, it's a sign, finding out about Angus. It's more than luck, finding someone else gets the blame for what I do. It's divine intervention, a sign I must go on.

But Angus is inside, he thought, they'll know he couldn't have done it.

They won't find her for weeks, he told himself, coming from where she does, no one will know she's missing for days. I can't turn back now.

She didn't wake when he stopped at his special place on the common. He went to the boot and took out a tarpaulin for her to lie on. He opened the passenger door to pull her out of the car, and then fell on to the ground sheet.

This is madness, he told himself, but it didn't matter. He was all powerful, he could outwit the cops, he would never be caught. They'd never even got close to him, even before they'd discovered Angus.

All I've got to do is get Angus out so he could've done this, he thought. I can do that, I can do anything, I have the power, I can . . .

And then he slowly, softly, started to punish the comatose child for being a bad little girl who would grow up to inflict unbearable pain on her helpless victims.

NINETEEN

Sarah had been awake most of the night, lying rigid in bed because the last thing she wanted was to wake Jeff and have to explain what was bothering her. The sight of Angus in that soulless visitors' centre in that awful place had upset her deeply. His situation seemed so hopeless, a kind of manifestation that Fate had it in for him and was enjoying itself mocking him. Worst of all had been his apparent refusal to see how helpless he was. She thought, he thinks they'll realize they've made a mistake and let him go home, he believes that.

She knew that was not going to happen. She tried to convince herself that if the police did discover they were wrong, they would admit it. She couldn't believe they would, though; things had gone too far now. They were under pressure from the media and the public to convict a child-killer, anyone would do if they could make a case against him. And the newspapers would fuel public opinion to do the rest.

In the morning, bleary-eyed, Sarah sat at her desk in the Savill's office and tried to pretend that she was interested in a technical question about the potential subsidence danger on a new site where a client wanted to build near old mine workings.

It was an important decision with hundreds of thousands of pounds riding on her findings. But she couldn't concentrate.

Finally, she got up to go to the coffee machine in case caffeine could help.

Neil followed her into the staff restroom where the coffee machine was. Sarah was annoyed, she wanted to be alone, but Neil had been in a chatty mood with everyone all morning and she knew she wasn't going to get rid of him without being rude.

'Don't tell me what you're having,' he said, 'let me guess. Double espresso, my treat.'

She couldn't refuse. It wasn't his fault that she felt as she did. Maybe he could make her feel better.

'Anything black,' she said, 'black and strong.'

He carried the coffee cups to a sofa near a window overlooking the courtyard garden behind the offices.

'What's up?' Neil said, settling himself beside her. 'Jeff playing up?'

'Jeff?' she said, puzzled. For a moment she couldn't think who he was talking about. 'Oh, no,' she said, remembering, 'nothing to do with Jeff.'

Neil laughed. 'You sound as though you'd never heard of him,' he said.

'How's your mother?' she asked.

'Still away staying with her friend. Don't change the subject. What's the matter with you?' Neil said.

'Oh, I went to see someone in prison yesterday. I've never been in a place like that before, it upset me, I suppose.'

'Angus Dillon?' he asked.

Of course he knows it must be Angus, she told herself, who else would I know in jail?

Sarah gave up trying to drive him away. He wasn't going anywhere, she knew him well enough to see that.

She nodded. 'Yes,' she said, 'Angus.'

'How's he doing?' Neil said. He sounded as though he cared, and Sarah remembered that he was involved with Joan and might be able to influence Angus's wife to try to help him.

She said, 'Angus was at home when Tara Davidson was killed, but he hasn't got an alibi. Honestly, Neil, it's awful, a perfectly innocent man spending a weekend at home, and suddenly there's this ridiculous accusation and he has to start proving he didn't do a particularly horrible crime. Can't you make Joan help? She could confirm his alibi. It's the least she could do.'

'Because of me, you mean?' Neil said. 'No can do, I'm afraid, the cops have already asked me and I confirmed she was with me. She can't go back on that now, can she?'

'No,' Sarah said, 'I suppose not.'

There was a pause, then Neil said, 'There is something you can do, you know.'

'No,' she said, 'I've spent all night thinking of ways of getting him out and there's nothing I can do.'

'Well, there you are, you see, the outsider does see most of the game. I've only thought about it for two minutes and it seems pretty obvious to me.'

Sarah searched his face for a sign that he was teasing her. It would be just like Neil to be sending her up when there was so much at stake. But he seemed perfectly serious.

'Well, what is it?' she said, preparing to shoot down any suggestion he had to make. Angus's wife was moving in with the man, for God's sake, why would he want to help get Joan's husband back on the scene? This time, she thought, perhaps he really is in love. He's never had anyone live with him before.

'You could give Angus an alibi,' Neil said.

Sarah stared at him, taking in what he'd said.

'It's simple,' Neil said, putting up his hands as though to ward off her expected grateful hug. 'You go to the cop in charge and you admit that you were scared because Angus was a married man, so you didn't say anything at the time because of keeping it a secret from Joan, but you were with him at the cottage all weekend.'

Sarah was still gaping at him like an idiot, so he said, 'After all, you couldn't know then that Joan was planning to leave him, could you? Your first instinct would naturally be to keep your illicit weekend quiet.'

'It won't wash,' Sarah said, 'they wouldn't believe Angus would keep a thing like that quiet if it got him out of a murder charge.'

'Of course he would,' Neil said, 'the man's a gent, one of the old-fashioned kind. He'd keep you out of it whatever happened.'

'They'd never believe me,' Sarah said.

'They might question your sanity, a young girl like you getting herself involved with a middle-aged has-been like Angus, but if they can't prove you're lying they've got to believe you. And they'll understand why you lied.'

'Why? Why did I lie?'

Neil gave her a pitying look. 'That's easily explained,' he said. 'Because of Jeff, you idiot. Isn't Jeff the reporter on the case? He's got a head start finding out your dirty little secret. Anyone could see why you had to be economical with the truth. But now you can't see an innocent man go to jail, you've decided you've got to risk losing Jeff and tell the truth.'

'My God,' Sarah said, 'you know it might work. If the DNA evidence is only circumstantial, they couldn't hold him if he's got a watertight alibi, could they?'

'I don't know, love, I've never understood the policeman's mindset. But with any kind of a lawyer . . .'

'Neil, you're a genius,' Sarah said, jumping to her feet. She was about to rush away but she turned back to ask, 'Did you really come up with that on the spur of the moment?'

Neil preened himself. 'Darling, it's not a question that's been exercising *my* mind all night, why should it? But I couldn't bear to see you looking so miserable, could I? I'm glad I could help, even though the lovely Joan may not thank me for it.'

'Bugger Joan,' Sarah said. 'Cover for me, will you? Say I've gone for an early lunch.'

The door of the restroom slammed behind her. Neil poured the coffee she hadn't drunk into his own cup.

He mimicked Sarah: 'Neil, you're a genius, did you *really* think of something so brilliant on the spur of the moment?' Then he began to sing softly, '*It's easy, it's so easy, like taking candy from a baby . . .*'

TWENTY

Neil spent most of the afternoon on site with new clients, a couple who wanted to convert the half-derelict buildings of an abandoned farmyard into a development of family homes, with state-of-the-art energy-saving technology built in.

The meeting went well.

As he prepared to leave, Neil said, 'I'll get my colleague Sarah Makepeace to contact you. She's an expert in feasibility studies and cost projections for this sort of thing.'

'Great,' the husband said. He shook Neil's hand. 'Good to see established architects who put their money as well as their mouths into society's future needs.'

'We pride ourselves on being ahead of the game,' Neil said. 'Sarah will be able to answer all your technical questions.'

The wife gave Neil a hard look as she said, 'We'll think about it.'

Neil understood at once that she didn't like the idea of another woman being involved. Until then, she had been telling him how she expected that she and her architect would be partners in creating dream homes for lucky families. Neil moved close to her and in a conspiratorial whisper said, 'If Sarah and your husband concentrate on the scientific stuff, you and I can get down to working together on the creative side, right?'

She simpered, quite won over.

It's in the bag, Neil told himself as he watched them drive off the site.

In his car, he rang the office to say his meeting was running late, he would go straight home when it was over.

'Joan Dillon has been trying to reach you,' the receptionist told him. 'She said it's *very* urgent and will you *please* ring her.'

'If she rings again, tell her I won't be back,' Neil said.

'I've told her already,' the receptionist said, 'I don't think she believes me.'

The girl was laughing at Joan, Neil could tell that. It struck him in passing that Joan seemed to have a knack of antagonizing other women. Sarah too appeared to have taken a dislike to her.

'Sorry,' Neil said meaninglessly to the receptionist.

'Oh, I'm used to it,' the girl said. 'It's not as if she's the first, is it?'

Neil wasn't sure if she was cheeking him or not. He laughed and put down the receiver.

Held up in a long line of traffic at roadworks, he checked the messages on the mobile phone. There were several missed calls from Joan. Irritated, he turned the phone off.

At Heart's-ease House (what a stupid name, he thought, the place was made to be Acacia Villa) he parked beside his mother's dilapidated pick-up. He had returned it to exactly its previous position on the gravel in front of the house after his trip to the Walker Estate. He prided himself on his meticulous attention to detail. Now he said to himself, once it's dark, I'll scrub it inside and out. I'd better not take it round the back and use the power hose, someone might notice it was moved and think Ma's been home, and we can't have anyone thinking that, can we?

He could hear the sound of Nellie snoring as he climbed the stairs. Not my idea of keeping the old girl quiet, he thought, but he was pleased, the drugs must still be having an effect. He hadn't been quite sure about what dose to give her. There wasn't much chance of anyone hearing her shouting if she'd woken up, but best not to risk it.

He unlocked her bedroom door and went in, saying in a cheery voice, 'Time to wake up, Ma. How are you feeling now? Have you had a good sleep?'

Nellie's eyelids flickered and she stared at him with blank unfocussed eyes.

He went to her and shook her by the shoulder.

'Wake up, Ma,' he said, 'it's almost time for your next pills.'

She struggled to raise herself in the bed. 'Neil? Neil, is that you? What's the matter with me, why am I in bed?'

'You've got to rest, Ma. Don't you remember, the doctor came and said you've got to keep very quiet for a few days. He gave you pills to take.'

'Doctor? What doctor? I don't remember any doctor.'

'Don't be silly, of course you remember. He came this morning. You told him you hadn't spent a day in bed since the day I was born and you weren't going to start now. But he said you'd got to stay quiet and rest, and you'll be right as rain in a day or two.'

'But what's *wrong* with me?' she insisted. 'Wasn't there something I had to do? Something important. Something about your brother Angus.'

Neil was irritated by the frail, whining tone in her voice. Damn, he thought, she hasn't forgotten that Angus business, she's still going on about telling the police he's her son. If their evidence against Dillon has anything to do with DNA, I can't let her go and blab that I'm their child-killer's twin, they might start asking questions. I'm going to have to shut her up.

He had no doubt that Sarah would follow out his instructions to the letter. So Angus would soon be out on bail, even if he was kept under surveillance. Released to kill again, Neil told himself, it happened all the time. Once Angus was in circulation, it wouldn't matter when they found the body of that girl from the Walker Estate. He'd dug a deep grave this time; she might not be found for a long time. The longer the better, up to a point. It made it more difficult to be too exact about the time of death. No one even seemed to have noticed she was missing yet. There hadn't been any mention of it on the lunchtime news he'd listened to on the car radio.

Not to worry, he said to himself, the cops will know where to go for their killer. And they won't think of looking further afield when Nellie turns up dead. Having Nellie claiming to be your mother would be enough motivation for anyone to murder her.

Neil laughed aloud. He was feeling pleased with himself.

In the meantime, though, he had to keep Ma quiet until Angus was out. Before long he'd be running out of the barbiturates. A doctor in Auckland had given them to him a while ago when he wasn't sleeping and he'd held on to them. But it would be dangerous to go to the local quack for another prescription. If it comes down to it, he told himself, I'll have to finish her off with one single overdose.

But that complicated things. Even if everyone assumed it was a confused old woman taking an accidental overdose, there were bound to be questions. Neil didn't want questions.

It suddenly occurred to him that maybe Nellie had papers proving her claims about Angus. If these existed, he should destroy them. Then he'd be in the clear. Nellie had come to England to search for Angus, she must have had something to make him believe her if she found him. She couldn't just march up to a strange middle-aged man and say 'You are my long-lost son and I claim my maternal rights.' Even Angus would want proof. Ma's not rich, Neil thought, she's not famous or anything, she's not someone anyone would want to claim as a mother unless she really was.

He had an idea.

He sat down on the bed and took her hand. 'Listen to me and don't get excited. Promise you won't get worked up. I've something to tell you, about Angus.'

She clawed at his arm. 'What? What about Angus?'

'I'm trying to tell you. But you're going to have to be a good girl and not get overexcited. Angus is coming to see you.'

Nellie was not so doped that she couldn't take this in.

Her eyes shone and she took Neil's hand and kissed it.

'Oh, thank you, thank you. He's coming here? Are you sure? Wasn't there something wrong, some problem? I seem to remember . . .'

'A mistake, that's all. The police thought he'd done something he didn't do. They've released him and he's coming to see you. He'll be here soon. But he's going to want to see proof, isn't he? He's not going to be convinced you're his mother without some kind of evidence.'

Nellie frowned, trying to concentrate through the rising fog in her head.

'I'll know him when I see him,' she muttered and smiled.

'Sure you will,' Neil said, 'but don't forget this is all new to him. He'll want proof.'

Then Nellie started to struggle, trying to kick back the duvet. 'I must get up,' she said, 'he mustn't see me like this.'

'No,' Neil said, 'you know what the doctor said. You've got to stay quiet. Otherwise I'll tell Angus he can't see you, he'll have to come back later, when you're better. I'll get the papers you've got to show him. Tell me where they are.'

She shook her head. Then she said, 'I'm nervous. Suppose he blames me? Maybe he'll hate me. He may've hated me all this time.'

'He didn't know you exist, Ma, he can't have hated you,' Neil said.

Nellie moaned. 'Oh God, what am I going to say to him?'

'I don't know. You'll think of something. Come on, Ma, pull yourself together.'

'I can't do this,' Nellie said, beginning to cry, 'I'm too scared of what he'll think of me.'

'Well, he won't be impressed if you're all blotchy from weeping,' Neil said brutally. 'You're supposed to be happy.'

He watched her, fascinated. What must she be feeling, convinced she was about to meet a son she'd dumped as a newborn baby? He and Angus were in their forties now; it was a long time ago. Why hadn't she let it go, forgotten all about him? What kind of life had she had, obsessed like that with . . . well, what, exactly? It couldn't be love, even if she told herself it was. Love, he told himself, had to have an object more tangible than something her body had discarded and she had left behind like a pile of shit. Curiosity? Guilt? That must be it, guilt. But what did she think she was going to get from finding Angus? Forgiveness, absolution? Did Angus even know he was adopted? Often kids weren't told in those days.

Does it even occur to her how selfish she's being? Neil wondered. How's Angus going to feel, having all that dumped on him? And has she ever thought for a moment about me, about how I might feel? He stared at his mother. She was trembling, her lips quivering and her hands unsteady.

What do *I* feel? he thought, I've been an only child all my life and suddenly there's not just a brother, but a twin.

Neil tried to imagine what it would have been like to be one of two when he was small, then as a teenager, now as an adult. No, he thought, I never wanted that, I'm glad he wasn't there.

But aren't I curious? he asked himself. Is he like me? What would it be like to see myself in another person? Would we think alike on important things? Or like the same people and dislike others. No, he thought, I'm not curious. I'm who I am and that's enough for me; I'm not interested in variations on the theme.

Of course, he had met Angus, and he'd felt no instinctive pull of shared heredity; the man was a stranger. I didn't like or dislike him, Neil thought. Then he told himself, he disliked me though, I'm sure he did. But that could have been because of Joan, he could see she fancied me. My brother's wife? Isn't that some sort of taboo, like breaking one of the Ten Commandments? Whatever, Angus hadn't seemed to fancy her particularly, so it's not even a sign we like the same women. Joan must've been in love with him once, of course, so perhaps they attracted the same women. Except, Sarah apparently liked Angus and was indifferent to him. Does he . . .? No, Neil thought, Angus wouldn't, he was too bloody straight, he'd be dead against any kind of perversion. But that's not heredity, it's probably more to do with childhood and the way you're brought up.

Even the physical characteristics, which Neil recognized now that he and Angus had in common – their eye colour, for one, and the basic shape of their features – seemed different because their different lives had changed them. They were probably the same height, Neil thought, but Angus was thin to the point of gauntness. I'm not, he thought, I'm what forensic pathologists call 'well-nourished', excessively well-nourished.

And he was suntanned and blonde where Angus's skin was pallid and his hair darker. Angus looked, Neil thought, like an old plant discarded in a dark place, where it had tried to develop without benefit of sunlight. He looks years

older than me, he told himself, and he's never had his teeth
capped. He's a wreck. No one would even think we could
be twins.

But now that he knew Nellie's story, Neil could see that
he and Angus were twins, identical twins. They were like
one actor playing different parts, in different costumes,
different make-up, different accents, but the same person.

He asked his mother, 'Why didn't you ever tell me about
him? You never said anything. Were we identical twins?'

It was a rhetorical question, he thought Nellie was unconscious. But she looked him in the eye and he realized
that she was seeing him clearly. The dope had worn off, it
was time to put her under again.

She said, 'I haven't seen him since he was an hour old,
all babies look alike to me.'

'But you chose me,' Neil said. 'You took me and you
left him, you must have made a choice?'

'You were nearest, I suppose,' Nellie said, and her eyes
clouded over again.

Neil wanted to hit her then. And he hated Angus, who
would expect to take a share of Nellie's love. He'd have
claims on her house and land, and on everything she had.
Why should he? Neil asked himself, why should he muscle
in now? He never put the time in being her son, but I did.
I've earned having my own mother to myself. I'm what she
made me. He isn't. If she doesn't like the way I am, she's
not going to move on to him and start again. I'm not having
that. She's mine, and what's hers is mine, I'm not going to
share what's coming to me.

He took the glass of water on the bedside table and held
it to Nellie's pale lips, pushing two pills into her mouth.
'Here's your medication,' he said, 'drink this. Angus will
be here soon.'

When she had swallowed them, he put down the glass.
Then, as though at a sudden thought, he said, 'Tell me
where the papers are, and I'll fetch them for you.'

'No,' she said, 'no papers. I want Angus.'

'And Angus you shall have,' he said. Let her show the
papers to Angus now, his brother would never see them.

He sat on the bed watching Nellie as the pills began to take effect. He saw unconsciousness slowly wash over her face like an outgoing tide across grey sand, wiping away the awareness in her eyes and the expression on her mouth.

She started to mumble and he took her by the shoulders. When he spoke to her he imitated Angus's slightly countrified English accent.

'Mother,' he said, 'at last. This is your son, Angus.'

This is ridiculous, Neil thought, what the hell is a middle-aged man supposed to say to a mother who abandoned him when he was a few hours old and comes back into his life more than forty years later? Not that she's hearing a word of it.

Nellie seemed to be struggling to take in what was happening. She clutched Neil's hand and tears coursed down her cheeks. 'Angus?' she mumbled.

Neil tried to maintain Angus's slightly burred English vowel sounds. 'Mother? It's really me.'

Nellie peered at him, trying to see more clearly.

She said in a faint, shaky voice, 'You looked so thin on the TV, I . . .'

Neil, in Angus's voice, said, 'It was an old photo. I've put on weight since then. When that picture was taken, I'd had jaundice. I used to drink.'

'Like Vince . . . like poor Vince . . .'

For a moment, it seemed as though Nellie smiled. Then she slumped back against the pillows, her eyes open but unseeing as the drug overwhelmed her will to stay awake. Neil noticed how yellow the whites of her eyes were. She's like an old woman, he thought, she hasn't got much love and attention to spare. And remembering, he told himself she'd never had enough, not for him or Vince, anyway. Neil was angry that what should have been theirs had been wasted on a long-gone baby who didn't even know she existed.

And never would. Let Angus suffer now, Neil thought, let him pay the price for a brother he'll never know he had. No one is ever going to know about Angus Dillon and me.

TWENTY-ONE

'We've had to let Dillon out on bail,' Chief Inspector Gifford told Sergeant Knowles. 'Keep a tail on him.'

Joe Knowles made no effort to hide his expression of disapproval, but he didn't dare say what he was thinking, which was that his boss had taken leave of his senses.

'He's got a cast-iron alibi, for God's sake,' Gifford said, answering Knowles's unspoken comment. 'Miss Makepeace's testimony was a gift from the gods for Dillon's solicitor.'

'Why should we believe her? The alibi, I mean,' Knowles said. 'We know he's involved with her, she was with him when we arrested him. And she visited him the other day. They've cooked this up between them. Otherwise why's it taken her so long?'

'She says she was with him but she was afraid her boyfriend would find out. He's the crime reporter on the local rag. She stood to lose from telling us the truth.'

'The truth?' Knowles gave a snort of derision. 'What about the DNA? At least that's a scientific fact, a lot more reliable than that bloody woman's word.'

'But circumstantial, Sergeant, circumstantial. Dillon's solicitor isn't a fool.'

'A used handkerchief covered in snot and God knows what else matching Dillon's DNA *under* the body, for Christ's sake. What more do you want?'

'But not *on* the body. Not *in* the body. Under the body isn't proof positive. Maybe the crime scene just happened to be where Angus Dillon went to wank off when he had hay fever or something. I know, not likely. Perhaps he went back there to think about how he found Julie Makepeace, like visiting a grave. I don't know. Whoever killed that girl wore gloves, there's nothing conclusive on the body. Our suspect has an alibi from before Tara Davidson went missing till after she was found because Sarah Makepeace says he was screwing the arse off her in his cottage. What else can we do? We found her fingerprints and DNA there to support her story.'

Gifford shook his head and Knowles saw that his boss, too, was angry at what was happening. 'Anyway,' Gifford went on, 'it's not up to me. Whether or not we believe Miss Makepeace, established judicial procedure says he can go out on bail.'

'So we wait till he does it again to another poor kid and flush our careers down the pan, I suppose,' Sergeant Knowles said.

'My career, not yours,' Inspector Gifford said, 'you can always say you were only following orders.'

They glared at each other, then Sergeant Knowles dropped his eyes. 'Where is he now?' he asked.

'At home. Alone. No sign of the wife or the girl. His phone's bugged, and Evans and Carter are pretending to be a courting couple outside the gate.'

'The mind boggles,' Knowles said, and they both laughed.

TWENTY-TWO

Sarah was watching television when Jeff came home.
She heard his key in the lock, and waited, but he didn't do his usual thing of shouting 'Sarah, I'm home, where are you?' He came straight into the sitting room, snatched the TV remote out of her hand and turned off the programme she was watching.

Sarah said nothing. There wasn't any point. The expression on Jeff's face as he looked down at her left her in no doubt that he had heard what she'd done.

'I can't believe what you've done,' he said. 'What the fuck do you think you're playing at?'

'Jeff, this has nothing to do with you,' she said. She couldn't think of anything else to say. She hadn't any explanation to give him. She knew why she had lied to give Angus an alibi, but there was no way she could make anyone else see why she'd done it, most of all Jeff.

'What possessed you to give him a false alibi?' Jeff couldn't hide his indignation that her lie somehow reflected badly on his manhood. 'You've lied to the police, you could go to jail.'

Sarah was defiant. 'Who said I lied?' she said. 'You were on that rugby trip in Scotland with the Hunsteignton Hornets that weekend, remember?' She couldn't resist teasing him, but instantly wished she hadn't. She felt that with this small intimacy she was conceding that he had the right to participate in her decisions.

'This is serious,' he shouted at her. 'Don't you know what you've done?' Then he suddenly stifled his anger and instead sounded patronizingly reasonable, as though she had been in an accident and was suffering from concussion. 'Darling, that man killed a young girl, he's sick, he should be locked up for his own sake, let alone everyone else's.'

Sarah got up and went to the sideboard, opened a bottle of wine, and poured a glass first for herself and then for him. She put his on the coffee table in front of him.

'No,' she said, 'he didn't kill anyone. No one's listening to him. It's obvious the moment you talk to him he doesn't know anything about the girl or how she was killed – you know, any details. He doesn't even know enough to try to invent a cover story and lie about her. You know much more than he does. You're a reporter, you'd see that if you could talk to him. Someone has set him up and the only chance he's got of proving it is if he's not banged up.'

'So who do you think you are, his guardian angel? What do you think's going to happen now?'

Sarah made an effort to get Jeff on her side. 'It's a story that the police have released him, isn't it? The papers will ask questions, the police will have to try and find more evidence. You can't let it drop now. It gets things moving.'

Jeff looked at her in amazement. 'You mean you did this for me, to give me a scoop? Sarah, you're crazy.'

Sarah in turn was astonished at the construction he was putting on what she'd done.

She took a deep breath. 'I thought it wouldn't do you any harm,' she said, 'can't you see the headline: Reporter's Girlfriend Makes Sensational Confession in Child-Killer Case? You'll be a celebrity if you play your cards right.' It sounded feeble to her, an attempt at bravado. Jeff wouldn't fall for it.

'You mean you did this for me? You thought you were helping?'

She could see that he thought she had taken leave of her senses.

'Oh, yes, I thought I was helping,' she said. Her tone was bleak.

'But how are you going to feel when he kills another innocent child? For God's sake, Sarah, you of all people. You've been through it yourself, with Julie Makepeace.'

She hated him for that Makepeace. It was as though her own niece was just another case history to him, not personal at all. Julie was part of his family too, or she would be when he married Sarah as he planned.

'Yes,' she said, 'I have. And that's why I know Angus hasn't done anything wrong. I guess I'm not like the police and the media and all the bloody people who just want someone punished whether he did it or not, so they can feel better about being part of a human race which has bastards in it who can do things like abusing and killing children.'

Her voice rose hysterically and she put her hands over her face to stop herself saying any more.

'Like me, you mean?' Jeff said. The quiet way he spoke sounded ominous and, shocked, she uncovered her face to look at him.

'I don't know you,' he was saying, 'I don't even recognize you when you're like this. I'm going to tell the police you're lying, even if it means they'll charge you.'

'You weren't here,' she said. 'I'm sticking to my story and you can't prove I'm lying. You'll only make a fool of yourself.'

He looked at her as though she were speaking in a foreign language.

'What's got into you?' he said, and now what he said seemed more in sorrow than in anger. 'Is this some twisted maternal instinct making you feel sorry for a monster? If I didn't know better, I'd say you think you've fallen in love with this paedo.'

She stared down at her hands in her lap and made no attempt to argue.

Jeff went white. For a moment she thought he was going to hit her but instead he turned and walked away. She heard the front door slam as he left the house.

TWENTY-THREE

Angus sat in his favourite chair in the familiar sitting room and waited for the sense of peace which the cottage had always worked on him. But it wasn't working now.

The deep silence that in previous times of turmoil had brought him calm now deepened his loneliness. In recent days and, most of all, nights in custody, the painful din of people constantly around him had been disturbing and he had longed then, as for salve on a burn, for the cottage and particularly this room, this chair.

But it was no comfort now. He felt only the absence of Joan. He hadn't really hoped that he would find her here when he came home, but he was disappointed anyway. She had been there in his absence. She'd lighted a fire. All his burned-out hopes seemed to lie consumed among the charred logs and the silvery shroud of ash she'd left in the cold grate.

Angus stared out of the French windows across the unmown lawn. The grass was long enough to bend in the wind. He thought of some large dark furry animal being stroked by a giant unseen hand.

An unseen hand, he told himself, what unseen hand is doing this to me?

Because he accepted now that Sarah was right. He had been set up. Impossible as it seemed, it must be true. At first it had seemed to him as though the police were simply making a mistake; that they would realize it as they had before when they'd suspected him of killing Julie Makepeace. He had waited, passive, for them to acknowledge their fault. At the beginning he'd even taken a detached pleasure in the thought of rubbing their noses in having to apologize. He'd rehearsed phrases in his head that he would say to them about one false accusation being a misfortune, but to make the same mistake twice sounds more like carelessness; that sort of pompous put down. It gave him brief satisfaction to think of it at the time, anyway.

But this wasn't the same as it had been with Julie. This time they were convinced of his guilt. They'd hated letting him go and they hated him for what they believed he'd done. They were out to make him pay. He didn't take their antagonism personally; they had enough evidence to make a clinical judgement that he was guilty of the worst crime in their book. They believed in his guilt with their heads, not only their hearts.

When Sarah lied to give him an alibi, his first reaction had been to protest, to tell them it wasn't true. She was taking an enormous risk for him, why should she have to do that? He was innocent, it was preposterous that there seemed no way for him to prove it. He was appalled that Sarah had to lie to make it possible.

His eyes burned with tears as he thought of her. He cried very easily these days, he seemed to be losing control over himself as well as his life. And poor Sarah. Of all the people he knew, she was the one who was not naturally a liar. She must've hated doing it, but she'd done it anyway. Why should she act so out of character unless she cared what happened to him? Why should she care that much? But she had, and now he had to try to deserve her generosity.

He wondered if he should telephone her. The police, he thought, would be listening in to his calls. Would they interpret a call to Sarah, however non-committal his conversation with her, as a confirmation of a real relationship re-enforcing the alibi, or as proof of collusion? Angus didn't dare risk it, though there was nothing he wanted more than to talk to Sarah. He didn't want to make trouble for her. No, he thought, no telephone calls. I shan't make any, and if the damned thing rings, I won't answer it. There's no one except Sarah I'd want to speak to anyway.

Sarah had done what she did knowing that he had to fight his own cause because no one else would. He couldn't do that unless he were free to act.

She'd done it for him. It had to be for him. She trusted

him. So he accepted her sacrifice. The only possible way
for him to repay her was to act to vindicate himself.

But how? he thought. How do I go about it?

The silence in the room oppressed him. It was early
evening but there wasn't a sound. Even the birds had stopped
singing.

Method acting, Angus told himself, that's what I must
do. Act innocent and I will be innocent.

He didn't think it was quite as simple as that, but it was
a start. If he hid himself away as though he were guilty,
people wouldn't even consider he could be innocent. Act
naturally, he told himself, do what you'd normally do.

I'd be down the pub, he thought, and for a moment it
seemed exactly where he wanted to be, just an ordinary guy
perched on a bar-stool, reading the local paper over a pint
and listening to Bet behind the bar telling old Major Peters
about her coach trip to the Loire Valley. Instead of a pariah,
a man accused of killing a child – two children – who should
be locked up for life whether he'd been found guilty or not.
Angus smiled, imagining Jane Thwaite, her ancient Barbour
creaking with indignation, laying down the law: 'Lock him
up and throw away the key, that's what I say. Better safe
than sorry as far as our children are concerned.'

A magpie landed on the lawn, trim and smart, strutting
like a policeman on parade.

Bastard bird, Angus thought, it's taunting me. That's why
the birds stopped singing. He turned to look at the dead
fire. In the old days he'd have been out there shouting at
the magpies to leave the songbirds alone and stop robbing
their nests. There was no use in futile gestures, the bird
wasn't his enemy, it was only doing what it must to survive.

Angus had a real enemy, but why? Why was he doing
this, this enemy? Who is it? he asked himself. Who hates
me enough to frame me?

Angus stared at the arrogant magpie but he no longer
saw it. 'Is someone doing this to me for his own survival?'
he said aloud, and then, to himself: there's only one reason
why anyone would have to do this, it's obvious. Whoever
my enemy is, he must be the murderer.

TWENTY-FOUR

Joan slowed the car as she approached Neil's house. She still wanted time to think. She started to turn into the drive. Then at the last moment she lost her nerve and jerked the wheel back on to the road and drove on. Now I'll have to find somewhere to turn round and come back, she thought. I'm being stupid, I don't know what's the matter with me.

The last she'd heard from Neil was a message left with the receptionist at work to tell her that he would be out of town for a day or two assessing a site for a client.

'But didn't he say when he'd be back?' Joan asked the girl who'd taken the message. 'He must've said something.'

'He didn't say,' the girl said, giving her a curious look, and added, 'And I didn't ask.'

But he must be back by now, Joan told herself, why doesn't he call? Even if he's working on site somewhere in the depths of the country, surely he'd have managed to ring by now. It wasn't as though she hadn't left messages for him, ringing his mobile night and day. But it was always turned off.

She reversed into someone's gateway and drove back towards the hideous red-brick villa., Trying to justify her intention to call at the house knowing his mother would be there, Joan thought, I've a right to know, something could've happened. Neil told me he loves me, we love each other, I've got a right to know.

This time she did turn into the drive and stopped outside the house. There were no lights on that Joan could see, but the curtains upstairs were closed and she told herself that Nellie had been away in New Zealand; maybe she was jet-lagged and had gone to bed early.

Joan rang the doorbell. She heard the hideous musical chime play the opening notes of *Land of Hope and Glory*. She's going to hate me, Joan told herself, but Neil and I are a couple, she's got to understand I'm worried about him. She can't object to me asking.

There was no reply to the musical bell. She rang again, and listened through the letter slot. The tune echoed as though the house were empty, but it didn't sound right to Joan. She thought, something's happened to him.

She had to know. She wished she could ignore her certainty that something was wrong. All her instincts told her to go away and come back tomorrow in daylight. It was the dark that was spooking her. But if something had happened to Neil, or even to Nellie, an accident or something, she had to try to help. She's going to be my mother-in-law, Joan told herself, it may make her like me better.

She walked round to the back of the house. The scent of herbs grew stronger. Neil had said Nellie concocted potions and healing creams from plants; perhaps she was out working, gathering her medicinal plants by moonlight or whatever it was she did. There wasn't much moonlight tonight, though. Joan shivered, feeling herself in the presence of something she didn't understand.

There was a pickup parked near the back door of the house, but no sign of Neil's car. Perhaps he was still away. Someone must be in, though, the house was too far from anywhere for Nellie to have gone out without transport.

Joan went to the kitchen door and banged on it. The old woman could be deaf. Or she might spend her evenings in the kitchen. Joan remembered the soulless front room she'd seen the one time she'd been here before with Neil, when Nellie was away. She thought, I wouldn't spend my evenings in that place, not at any price.

Still there was no reply to her knock on the back door. She tried the handle and the door opened.

'Mrs Carver,' Joan shouted from the step, then, going inside, she called again, 'Nellie, where are you? Are you there?'

Silence. But not the silence of an empty house, more as though someone were listening. I'm being fanciful, Joan told herself.

'Nellie,' she said, 'are you all right?' She could hear the quaver of fear in her voice.

She found a light switch on the wall by the door and turned it on. The kitchen suddenly appeared, as clean and orderly as when she had last seen it. But there was an unwashed glass on the draining board. The woman who had created that mushroom and magnolia sitting room would never have gone to bed without washing a dirty glass.

'Mrs Carver,' she yelled, 'hold on, I'm coming.'

Joan wasn't sure what she was expecting. She turned on the lights as she searched, making as much noise as she could to give herself confidence. She was more and more certain as she moved through the immaculate downstairs rooms that there was something wrong.

Upstairs there was nothing in what was obviously Neil's room. The bathroom might never have been used. At least Nellie had not cut her wrists in the bath. Why did I think something like that? Joan asked herself. She realized that that was what she was afraid of, that Neil had told his mother about their plans to be together, and Nellie, left alone while Neil worked away, had reacted by killing herself.

The room at the top of the stairs was locked.

Joan knocked, then rattled the knob. She listened, her ear to the keyhole, and it seemed to her that she could hear something.

'Mrs Carver,' she called, 'let me in.'

Nothing. No sound at all now. And yet she had heard something.

She stood back, considering what to do next. Then, on a delicate glass-topped half-moon table against the wall beside the bedroom door, she saw a key.

She took it and tried it in the lock. It fitted. She turned the key and the door opened.

For a moment Joan was driven back by the wave of stale fetid air that engulfed her as she went into the room.

My God, she thought, the old woman's been dead for days and her body's decomposing.

She found herself whispering. 'Nellie?'

She turned on the light.

There was a gasp. Joan didn't know whether it came

from her, or from the skeleton who seemed to rise like a Halloween puppet on strings from the bed.

And then she realized that what she was looking at was an old woman, who looked at death's door, lying in bed and trying to pull herself up against the pillows.

Nellie's wispy grey hair hung loose. Her skin looked like cobwebs draped across the jagged cheekbones, shrouding the dark hollow sockets of her eyes.

Joan stared at her in horror. She wanted to turn and flee, but her feet were rooted to the floor.

'Please,' the old woman croaked from the bed, trying to reach out her hands.

She's dying, Joan thought. She had been in the presence of the dying before. Sometimes in the past clients had wanted to make last-minute additions to their wills, and Joan's bosses had considered that a job best done by a woman. Now she was a full partner in the firm it didn't happen so much. But she recognized the aura of lingering death and suddenly she was not afraid.

She went to the bed and took the old woman's hand. The bones felt like old straw in her grasp and she heard the rasp of Nellie's dried skin.

'What can I do?' Joan said. 'Where's Neil?'

'He'll be back,' Nellie whispered. 'He's coming back. Help me.'

Joan had to lean forward to hear the old woman's hoarse whisper.

'You need a doctor,' Joan said. 'I'll call an ambulance.'

She felt in her pocket, and cursed herself for leaving her mobile in the car.

'Where's the phone?' she asked.

Nellie shook her head. 'No, don't go,' she said. 'Wait.'

Joan found it hard not to gag as she leaned over the old woman, trying not to look at the loose withered skin or breathe the rancid air.

'I'll open the window,' she said.

She pulled her hand away from Nellie's bony grasp and drew back the curtains, throwing up the sash window and taking great grateful gulps of the cool night air.

'There,' she said, turning back to the bed, 'that's better. Now tell me what's happened. Are you ill?'

Nellie stared at her and slowly shook her head.

'Who are you?' she asked.

Joan hesitated. 'I'm a solicitor,' she said. Then she burst out, 'I'm in love with your son. We want to get married.'

'Angus?' the old woman said. 'You and Angus?'

Joan was startled. So Neil has told her about me, she thought, he must've said I'm married to a man called Angus. Is that what's driven her to this state, that Neil's breaking up a marriage?

'No,' she said, 'not Angus. Your son.'

'Angus is my son,' she said, 'he was here, he came to see me. Angus and Neil, twins, my twin sons.'

Joan, leaning over the bed to make out the feeble croaking voice, was suddenly aware of a look of terror in the old woman's sunken eyes as she stared over Joan's shoulder at something behind her.

Joan looked round to see what had frightened Nellie.

Neil was standing in the doorway. She had never seen him look angry before, but now she knew that he was furious. The skin around his compressed lips was white, his pale eyes like flint. He was staring at her as though he hated her – her or Nellie.

'What the hell are you doing here?' he asked.

'I was worried,' Joan said. 'You didn't ring, and you didn't answer my messages. I came to see your mother. I didn't know what else to do. I was afraid something had happened to you.'

Pretending bravado, she met his eyes and smiled. 'We've had a bit of a chat, your Mum and me,' she said. 'Is it true?'

'Is what true?'

'That Angus is your twin.'

Neil laughed. 'Oh, Ma, what have you been saying?' He turned to Joan, 'She's not quite in her right mind at the moment, you can see she's not well. She caught some infection when she was staying with her friend. The quack's given her pills.'

He walked across to the bed opposite Joan and took up the small brown bottle of pills on the bedside table. 'It's time for your next medication, Ma,' he said. 'I'll fill the glass so you can take your pills.'

He went to a wash basin near the window and turned on the tap. In the moment that his back was to the bed, Nellie suddenly took a much-folded envelope from inside one of her pillow cases and thrust it at Joan.

'Hide it,' she whispered. 'It proves what I said.'

Something fearful about her, the helpless way she seemed to be pleading, made Joan take the paper and slip it down the front of her bra. She thought, it's the least I can do if it makes her feel better.

'What did she say?' Neil said. He was back at the bed, holding a glass of water to Nellie's mouth and pressing a pill between her bluish lips.

'Nothing I could make out,' she said. 'I think she was just mumbling.'

'She'll sleep now,' Neil said, 'we'd better let her get some rest. That's what the doctor said. Come downstairs, we can talk there.'

He ushered her out of the room and closed the door behind them.

'The door was locked,' Joan said, 'she was locked in.'

Neil was unruffled. 'Only while I was out,' he said. 'The doctor suggested it in case she started to move about and fell downstairs. She's had a very high fever, she's been quite disorientated.'

Joan was convinced. It was reasonable enough. And Nellie was under a doctor, she wasn't dying at all, simply recovering from a nasty foreign infection.

She followed Neil into the kitchen.

'Drink?' he asked. 'I need a drink and so must you. Finding Ma like that must've been quite a shock. Water or soda with the Scotch?'

'Water's fine.'

He took her drink to the sink and added a splash of water from the tap.

'Cheers,' he said, handing it back to her.

'She said Angus is her son, you and Angus, her twin sons. Neil, is it true?'

'Joan, you saw the state she's in, how can you take any notice of some sort of fantasy she's got in her head. I mean, how could it be true? You've only got to look at us to know.'

Joan shook her head. 'But why should she say it? And actually, when it comes down to it, you do look alike. Why should she know anything about Angus? Did you tell her about us and mention him being my husband?'

'Of course not, why should I?' Neil said, and she could hear the irritation in his voice. 'How could we even be related? I was born in New Zealand and Angus is English. Isn't he?'

'I don't know,' Joan said. 'He was adopted, that's all I know.'

Neil's tone changed at that. 'Really, Angus was adopted? I didn't know that. Joan, you don't think there could be something in it, do you? We could be related, you know. Strip away the surface differences, we do look quite alike, I suppose.'

Joan could feel Nellie's folded envelope sharp against the skin of her breast inside her bra.

'There's proof,' she said, but she made no attempt to produce the paper. Why? she asked herself, what's holding me back?

Neil's eyes were suddenly wary.

'What do you mean, proof?' he asked. 'What proof?'

Joan thought, why am I afraid?

She said, 'Well, you could have a DNA test. That would show if you and Angus were related.'

He slammed his glass down on the kitchen counter, spilling whisky on to the gleaming granite surface.

'No,' he said through clenched teeth, 'no DNA. Nothing like that.'

'But why not? It's so simple. The police have Angus's DNA already. That's been his trouble, actually, years ago they matched him with something at the site of that poor child Julie Makepeace and now they're doing the same thing with this new murder, the teenage girl they found on the common.'

Neil refilled his glass and then hers, getting up to go to the tap for water.

'No DNA,' he said. 'Absolutely not.'

'But why not? It would tell you once and for all.'

Neil put the full glass in front of her and tipped her face to kiss her lips. 'Don't you see, you silly little thing? Suppose it's true and Angus and I are related. There's bound to be some sort of law against it, going with your twin brother's wife, that sort of thing. I'm not going to risk losing you like that, am I?'

The feel of his kiss on her mouth triggered the familiar surge of lust. She put up her arms to pull him towards her, making the stool she was sitting on rock dangerously. She stood up, then felt that she was melting at his feet. She laughed.

'All you have to do is touch me and my legs won't even hold me,' she whispered, 'please, Neil, make love to me.'

A voice somewhere in the back of her mind was saying over and over again, 'He's knows Angus is his twin, he doesn't want DNA to prove it. Why, if he wasn't the one who killed those girls?'

Don't be stupid, she told herself, of course he didn't. She couldn't listen to the insistent voice, not yet. As always, her body's pleasure swamped her mind. She pulled down her pants without undressing. His mouth was hot on hers, then swooning pleasure overwhelmed her as he entered her, and that was all.

TWENTY-FIVE

Sergeant Knowles replaced the receiver on the phone on Detective Chief Inspector Gifford's desk. He looked excited. Gifford asked, 'What's happened?'

'That's it,' Knowles said, with the expression of a man who wanted to give the high five to his boss but didn't quite dare. 'He's done it again.'

He looked expectantly at the Detective Inspector. Gifford's reaction disappointed him. He didn't even ask any questions, just looked thoughtful.

Knowles thought the boss hadn't understood the implications of the message. He said, 'That young girl they found on the refuse tip. She was strangled.'

Gifford nodded.

'Murdered,' Knowles insisted. 'You see what this means, Angus Dillon's at it again.'

'How long's she been dead?' Inspector Gifford said. 'Dillon's only been out a few days.'

'Impossible to tell exactly, but recent,' Sergeant Knowles said reluctantly. 'The rubbish tip makes it difficult. Affects the rate of decomposition, I guess.'

'Who is she?'

Knowles was impatient. He wanted his superior officer's go ahead to bring Angus Dillon in and start giving him the treatment. He said, 'We think she may be a girl from the Walker Estate, name of Sandra Perry. Cautioned for soliciting three months ago. Aged fourteen.'

His lack of interest in the details was obvious.

'How long's she been missing?' Gifford asked.

Knowles could hear the resigned concern in Gifford's voice. His own tone made it clear that he'd told his boss what would happen, and it had.

'We're not sure about that either,' Knowles said. 'This girl had moved away from home three months ago and was living in a squat on the Walker. No one reported her missing, but her mother saw her picture on television and came in. Stroke of luck, really, her recognizing the kid. The only picture we had was the one on the police file when she was arrested. Only a mother would recognize one of those.'

'DNA?'

'They're doing tests,' Knowles said. 'Want to put money on it?'

Gifford shook his head. 'What kind of monster are we dealing with?' he muttered.

For a moment Joe Knowles thought his boss was referring to him, but then he realized he was reacting to the child-killer.

'At least we know where to look this time,' he said, trying to cheer him up.

The phone rang again and this time Gifford answered it himself.

'When was this?' Gifford said into the telephone. He listened for a time, then he put down the phone and said to Sergeant Knowles, 'They've just fished Joan Dillon's body out of the river.'

Sergeant Knowles whistled through his teeth. 'Suicide?' he asked.

'Looks like it.'

'That clinches it, then,' Knowles said. 'We can use that on Dillon. It's obvious. Mrs D saw Sandra Perry's picture and knew that her husband had struck again. She couldn't bear the guilt, or face life as the ex-wife of a multiple child-killer so she took the pills with a few slugs of whisky and threw herself into the river.'

'Maybe,' Inspector Gifford said. 'Or our Angus topped her up with booze and pills and tipped her in the river. Whichever, she drowned. She may've been drunk and drugged to the eyeballs, but she was alive when she went in the water. That's been established, at least.'

'My God, that could be it,' Knowles said. 'Sandra Perry may've been the straw that broke the camel's back. Joan may've been going to spill the beans. So he stopped her.'

Inspector Gifford raised his eyebrows. 'Except he's been

under close surveillance and he hasn't been in touch with her,' Inspector Gifford said.

'Oh, that doesn't mean anything,' Knowles said airily. 'I've always suspected those kids we put on watch sleep most of the night.'

'Don't judge everyone by yourself, Sergeant,' Gifford said, but he didn't sound too serious.

'Maybe Evans and Carter got it on for real and were preoccupied,' Knowles said.

Inspector Gifford ignored that. 'I want to take a look at the body,' he said. 'I want to make sure it couldn't be murder. Let's get down there before they move the corpse.'

To get to the river, a tributary which was not significant enough to have an official name, they had to drive down a long track through steep banks overgrown with cow parsley.

For the first time, Knowles sounded doubtful. 'It's not the first place I'd think of to dump a body,' he said.

'You favour the suicide theory, then?' Gifford said. 'I suppose it's too much to hope that anyone noticed fresh tracks before all these bloody vehicles spoiled any chance of forensics?'

'I think she was found by a farmer checking stock. He might've noticed if anyone had used the road before him. He might've been on the lookout for cattle thieves.'

'What an exciting world you live in,' Inspector Gifford said, looking at Knowles with something like awe.

Joan Dillon's body was about to be bagged up. A group of young heifers had gathered to watch. Someone had tried to push them back behind scene-of-crime tape but they kept breaking through to sniff at the body. They've obviously never seen anyone wearing high heels before, Inspector Gifford told himself. They had trampled the grass, making a forensic search pointless.

Seeing Gifford and Knowles, the ambulance driver was defensive. 'This wasn't a crime,' he said, 'I've never seen a clearer case of suicide. She had stones in her pockets.'

'Anything on the body?' Gifford asked. 'No note?'

The local cops who had first been called to the body by the farmer looked at each other.

'There's this,' one said, handing Gifford a damp wad of paper.

'Have you read it?'

'No sir, we were going to take it back to the station and dry it out. We thought it might fall apart if we tried to read it. Not much doubt it's a suicide note, though.'

Inspector Gifford took the paper.

'It's drier than I'd have expected,' he said. 'Where did you find it?'

'It was inside her ... er ... brassiere, sir. I suppose she thought we'd be bound to find it there when it came down to it. Safer than leaving it around where it might not get noticed.'

It was a peaceful place to die, Gifford thought, the perfect picnic spot for a family, where the kids could swim and there were lots of birds and wild flowers. And litter, of course, there was always litter somewhere as nice as this.

He thought of Joan Dillon, who hadn't struck him as the type who'd kill herself. Surely she was happy with that new man of hers, he told himself, she didn't seem to me to associate herself that closely with Angus Dillon. Perhaps the boyfriend used Dillon's arrest and the reason for it to dump her, but even so. And this wasn't Joan Dillon's kind of place, anyway. She wasn't a country girl, she'd go to a hotel room with crowds close by.

Gifford sighed as he turned to go back to the car.

'We'd better inform Dillon and that boyfriend of hers,' he said. 'I suppose his name's on file, he made a statement saying he'd been with her the weekend Tara Davidson died, remember? Has anyone reported Joan Dillon missing?'

Knowles shook his head.

Back at the office Inspector Gifford was almost convinced, but there was still something at the back of his mind that worried him. For a start, how did a woman like Joan Dillon even know about that place? Also she was wearing ridiculously high heels and there was no sign of an abandoned car near the river. She'd never have walked all the way down that track to get there, not in those shoes.

He was about to call Knowles to get him to check local taxi firms who might've taken her to the river when his Sergeant burst into his office.

'Knocking, Sergeant?' Gifford said, the shorthand protest he made twenty times a day.

'They've got a reading on the suicide note on the Dillon body,' Knowles said. 'It's not what we expected.'

There's no point asking how he thinks he knows what I'm expecting, Gifford told himself. After all the time he and Knowles had worked together, he was weary of picking him up on all the little things the sergeant did that irritated him.

He took the paper on which forensics had typed the message, and started to read.

'What the hell is this all about?' he said.

'What it comes down to is that some old bird called Nellie Carver thinks she has reason to believe that Angus Dillon is the baby she apparently abandoned more than forty years ago and therefore the brother of her son Neil Carver.'

Sergeant Knowles intoned this as though he was more than half convinced that what he was reciting was the perverted fantasies of a senile woman.

'Who the hell is Nellie Carver?'

'Isn't Joan Dillon's boyfriend called Neil Carver? Maybe this Nellie woman is his mother.'

Inspector Gifford frowned. 'But why the hell did Joan Dillon hide that info in her bra as though it was a secret code or something. Did Nellie Carver give it to her, and if so, why?'

'Delusions of paranoia?' Knowles suggested.

'Or was the old woman afraid of something and gave it to Joan to keep it out of the hands of someone else?'

'Who could only be Angus Dillon,' Knowles said. 'That's the only possible explanation.' Knowles was beginning to get carried away with enthusiasm for the chase.

'Or Neil Carver,' Inspector Gifford said. 'That's a possibility. Except that surely if Joan knew what it said, she'd have told her lover Neil that Angus was his brother.'

'Like hell she would,' Knowles said. 'She's mad about Carver, she's not going to tell him something like that. She'd be afraid that's the last she'd see of him.' Then he added as an afterthought, 'Sir,' in case he'd sounded disrespectful.

Gifford got to his feet. 'I bow to your superior knowledge of the middle-aged female psyche, Joe,' he said. 'There's only one way of finding out. We've got to get to Mrs Carver. We need her to answer a few questions.'

TWENTY-SIX

As soon as he woke, Angus was sure that Joan was dead.

He lay in bed staring at the drawn curtains Joan had made when they first came to live at the cottage. Someone had given her the material, a thick cotton with a William Morris design called Daisy. Angus thought it was pretty.

I must've been dreaming, he told himself, of course she's not dead, why should Joan be dead?

But he couldn't shake off the certainty that something terrible had happened to Joan.

He got up and went downstairs to telephone his wife. She'll be cross at me ringing her so early, he thought, especially if she's with Neil. But that's too bad, I've got to make sure she's OK.

He dialled Joan's mobile number and then, listening to it ringing, had a moment of panic about what he was going to say to her when she answered. 'Oh, good, I was afraid you were dead' didn't seem quite right. He thought, I'll put the phone down when she answers. If she rings back, I'll say I dialled her accidentally. Joan wouldn't be surprised at that.

He took it for granted that she imagined she still occupied all his thoughts.

Then a male voice answered, 'Hello.'

'Is that you, Neil?' Angus asked. He was taken aback that anyone but Joan should answer her mobile.

'This is Detective Constable Jackson, Hunsteignton police. Who is this, please?'

Angus hesitated. Then he said, 'I'm trying to contact my wife. I'm Angus Dillon. Have I dialled the wrong number, this should be her mobile? Where are you, anyway?'

It doesn't mean she's dead, he told himself, she could have had an accident, or had her phone stolen.

Constable Jackson said, 'I'm sorry to have to tell you, sir, but I'm in the police morgue and your wife is deceased. The telephone was with her body.'

For a moment Angus thought he had been struck blind. The world went black around him. His brain, like his hands, seemed turned to ice. And yet he wasn't surprised. What seemed most shocking was finding that his horrible premonition was real. He was terrified that he was responsible, that he had brought about her death as some kind of vengeful wish fulfilment.

'My God,' he managed to gasp, 'how?'

He could almost hear the constable backtracking across the ether. He sounded very young. 'You're Mr Dillon?' he said, 'Mr Angus Dillon?'

Jackson sounded appalled at what he had done.

Angus was suddenly thinking very clearly. He told himself, the boy's suddenly realized what he's done, he thinks he's given away something he shouldn't.

The young constable was stammering, 'I'm very sorry, sir, I'm sure Inspector Gifford's on his way to see you. I know he left the office. I thought you'd been told. I didn't think.'

'How did she die?' Angus asked, but in a way he knew that, too. She'd died a violent death, by unnatural causes, she must've done or why would the police have her phone?

'I can't say, sir, I'm sorry,' Jackson said. He sounded pathetically embarrassed. He added, 'I'm sure Inspector Gifford . . . I'm just the man on the desk, I don't know anything really.'

Angus put down the phone. His legs felt weak and he held on to the back of an armchair as he made his way to the sideboard and took a slug of whisky straight from the bottle. Then he filled a glass and drank that, too.

He took the bottle with him and went to sit beside the dead fire, staring at the silvery ash as though Joan, who had once lighted the logs, was still present in some kind of essence in the burnt wood. Certainly, he thought, the cottage now felt empty as it had not before, it was as though he only imagined that she had ever lived there with him.

He got up at last and went to open the front door so that Inspector Gifford and his sidekick could come straight in when they arrived. Let them barge in as they usually did, he had no intention at all of ever willingly inviting them into his home.

They think I had something to do with it, he thought. That's what made that young cop realize he'd put his foot in it, telling me.

'Oh, Joan, I'm so sorry,' he said, speaking aloud as though she were there with him in the room, 'I thought that at last you might've found a little happiness.'

Poor Joan, who was so terrified of physical pain. There were so many things she'd never done in case she hurt herself. Like when he'd tried to teach her to ride a horse, or bought roses to plant around the cottage porch and she'd cried when she caught her finger on a thorn.

I hope it didn't hurt, he thought, whatever happened to you.

Slowly, he got up and went upstairs to dress. When that thug of a sergeant and his boss arrived, he was going to be ready for them.

TWENTY-SEVEN

'Doesn't look as though the old bat's up yet,' Sergeant Knowles said, parking the car in the drive at Heart's-ease House. 'Maybe she's out,' he added. 'There's no sign of a car.'

There was no reply when they knocked at the front door. Knowles went round to the back and called to Inspector Gifford, who was following him, 'There's a pickup here.'

He pounded on the door, shouting 'Open up, police,' but still there was no sign of life from the house.

'What now, sir?' Knowles asked.

'She might be in danger,' Inspector Gifford said. 'We've reason to believe she could be.'

'Nod's as good as a wink to a blind man,' Knowles said.

Inspector Gifford was startled at the sudden movement as Knowles stepped back from the door and then lifted one hefty leg and aimed his boot at the lock. The wood splintered and the door snapped open. It crossed Gifford's mind that it might not have been locked, they hadn't tried to open it.

Knowles rushed through the house like a massive terrier after a rat. He climbed the stairs two at a time, leaving muddy footprints on the pale carpet. Gifford followed more slowly. There was something about the house that puzzled him. He'd glanced into the kitchen and the tasteful sitting room which looked like a show home. There were no family photos, no framed snapshots, no knick-knacks, nothing personal at all. Where's Neil Carver in all this? he asked himself. Maybe the mother's houseproud, but what about him, it's like he's invisible.

He heard Knowles call, 'Sir.' Something in the Sergeant's voice made Gifford hurry up the rest of the stairs and into a bedroom that Knowles had plainly entered the same way he'd come into the house.

Knowles was beside the bed, checking the emaciated woman who lay there for signs of life.

'She's not dead,' he said. 'I can feel her pulse. Perhaps she's drunk.'

Gifford took a quick look. 'That's not drunk,' he said, 'call an ambulance. Are there signs of violence?'

Suddenly the woman on the bed opened her eyes and stared around the room, apparently not recognizing where she was. Gradually her eyes focussed on the two men.

'Who are you?' she demanded, and her voice was surprisingly strong. 'What are you doing here? Where's Neil?' She turned to Gifford. 'Are you the doctor?'

'Is your son Neil here, Mrs Carver?' Gifford asked.

Nellie frowned. 'It's so cold in here. I've been asleep a long time.' The old woman struggled to sit up in the bed. 'Neil didn't give me my pill last night,' she said. 'The doctor said I had to take my pills regularly but he forgot. They're on the table.'

She pointed a wavering finger at a small brown bottle on the bedside table. Knowles picked it up and held it at arm's length to read the label.

'Luminal,' he said. 'That's phenobarbital, isn't it? Why would she be prescribed that?'

'Perhaps she's epileptic,' Gifford said. 'Are you?' he asked Nellie.

She seemed not to understand what he was talking about.

Knowles tipped the remaining pills into the palm of his hand. There were only three of the small white tablets left.

'Hey,' he said, 'the chemist who dispensed these was in New Zealand.'

'Where is your son, Mrs Carver?' Inspector Gifford said.

'How should I know? He came here after you let him out of jail, but he's not here now.

'Who was here?' Gifford asked. He looked puzzled. 'We've never had Neil Carver in jail, why should we?'

Nellie appeared to be drifting off again. 'Not Neil, Angus,' she said. 'And then there was a woman, she was nice. Joan, that's what Neil called her. Or Jane, or Jean, something like that.'

The two policemen exchanged glances.

'Joan?' Gifford asked. 'Joan came here?'

Nellie smiled and shook her head.

'Neil wasn't pleased,' she said. 'He took her away. He likes to keep his women to himself.'

'Away?' Knowles asked.

Nellie blinked, as if trying to clear her eyes. 'Well, he took her downstairs,' she said. 'He didn't like her talking to me, I could tell. But it was nice to have a woman to talk to for a change.'

They heard the distant sound of an ambulance siren approaching the house.

'I'll try to stall them,' Knowles said, moving towards the bedroom door.

'No,' Gifford said, 'look at her, for God's sake, she should be in hospital. We're not going to get anywhere talking to her the way she is. She's probably off her head, we can't believe a word she says till she's had her stomach pumped or whatever they have to do to get that stuff out of her system.'

'What about bringing Angus Dillon in?' Knowles asked. 'There's something going on here. Why should Dillon come to see her? Do you think he gave her an overdose of these pills?'

'Let's leave him be till we know more about what's going on,' Gifford said. 'We don't want any more mistakes. He's not going anywhere. We've got to know what we're asking him.'

Knowles looked disapproving, thinking his boss was going soft.

'I hope you're right,' Knowles said. 'But he seems to have visited the old bat without us knowing anything about it. That's not the action of an innocent man.'

Inspector Gifford nodded. 'We'll have to check on that. You get on and do it, Sergeant. Did he really visit Nellie Carver, or was it the drug talking?

'Or is she just doolally?' Sergeant Knowles said, his tone making it plain that that's what he thought.

'The one I really want to talk to first is Neil Carver,'

Inspector Gifford said. 'If Joan Dillon was here, in this house with Nellie, Neil could be the last person who saw her alive, maybe he's some idea where she was going. He'd know what sort of state she was in, too.'

'Perhaps the old girl said something about Neil's record with women which sent Joan over the edge,' Knowles said. 'Or maybe Neil was so angry with her he sent her packing. That could do it, if she thought she was in love with him.'

'Maybe, but why should he be so angry?' Gifford said. 'But apart from that, Neil's the one who's going to be able to shed some light on what's been happening to Nellie, don't you think?'

'Isn't she something for social services to deal with?' Knowles said. 'Not the police, and certainly not CID, wouldn't you say?'

'No, Sergeant,' Gifford said sternly, 'that's not what I'd say at all.'

TWENTY-EIGHT

S arah heard Jeff come into the house and she grabbed a magazine which she pretended to read. Since the time he'd slammed out in a huff and stayed away all night, the two of them had tried to avoid any direct contact.

But tonight was different. Jeff started to shout for her the moment he'd banged the front door. She heard him hurrying through the hall shouting her name.

She got up and opened the sitting room door. 'I'm in here,' she said, very cool.

Jeff ignored her. The words tumbled out of his mouth, he was in such a hurry to tell her. 'Have you heard the news about Angus Dillon?' he demanded.

'What about Angus?' she said, deliberately making herself sound uninterested.

Jeff grinned. 'Only that his wife's dead. What about that? Someone's topped her.'

Sarah stared at him. 'Are you sure?' she said.

'Sure I'm sure,' Jeff said. 'A friend who works at the morgue told me the gory details. She took an overdose and drowned herself, that's what they think.'

'That's not murder, that's suicide?'

My God, Sarah thought, Joan can't have killed herself. Why should she do that? She didn't give a damn what was happening to Angus. She was happy, she'd got Neil.

Jeff shook his head, enjoying taunting her with information he knew she couldn't wait to hear, however much she tried to pretend she wasn't interested. 'Not necessarily,' he said, teasing her, 'they haven't ruled out foul play.'

Sarah turned away. She wasn't going to go along with his childish game.

'Really?' she said.

She sat down and picked up the magazine she had been pretending to read.

Jeff followed her and snatched it.

'Listen,' he said, 'this is something hardly anyone knows . . .'

'A little friend who works in forensics told me . . .' Sarah said, imitating him. Then she thought, please God, don't let them find some way of pinning this on Angus.

Jeff said, 'It was a nurse at the hospital, actually. Apparently, the mother of that bloke Neil who works at your office is claiming that your precious Angus is a long-lost son she's been searching for all these years.'

'That's ridiculous, it can't be true. Your nurse friend's having you on.'

'The mother was brought into the hospital suffering from some sort of overdose. Odd that, another overdose—' He broke off for a moment, frowning, then went on. 'Sonia – that's my friend – heard the doctor on duty talking about what she'd said.'

Sarah looked stunned. Watching her face, Jeff suddenly seemed to realize what he had actually said. He suddenly sat down beside her on the sofa as though someone had hit him.

'What a story,' he said, and then hesitated. 'If it's true.'

'Perhaps she had an illegitimate child before she married Neil's father and never dared tell him. That happened a lot in those days.'

There was a short silence while they both tried to digest the implications of the information.

'Do you think it could be true?' Jeff asked.

Sarah started to dismiss the story. True, that night of the dinner party at the Dillon cottage, she'd noticed something, some similarity between Neil and Angus. It was more than simply that, if you took away the obvious facts that Neil was plump and pampered and carefully groomed and Angus was gaunt and pale and had five o'clock shadow, they had similar bone structure and colouring. There were little mannerisms, the way they picked up a glass, or slightly cocked their heads when they were listening to what someone was saying. Joan had noticed it. She'd said something. Sarah tried to remember. Something about Neil reminding her of Angus when she'd first known him, before all his troubles. She'd said Neil was like the Angus she'd fallen in love with. She'd told Neil that, he'd mentioned it afterwards. He'd thought it was a line. Perhaps Joan spoke truer than she knew . . .

Jeff was watching Sarah.

'You think it could be true, don't you?' he said.

'That they're brothers?' Sarah nodded, but she sounded doubtful as she said, 'I don't know. There are things that fit. I know Angus was adopted, he makes no secret of it. And Joan said something . . .'

'You don't think Joan *knew*, do you?'

Sarah got up quickly. The magazine slipped off the sofa on to the floor but they both ignored it.

'No, of course she didn't know,' she said, 'but there was something about Neil that reminded her . . . she mentioned it. Neil told me afterwards. He thought it was funny, but it scared him, I think, he felt threatened by her. I just assumed he thought she was coming on too strong and he wanted her to cool it.'

'So Neil didn't know?'

Sarah thought for a moment. Then she said, 'No, I'm sure he didn't. He can't have.'

She was thinking, if Neil had known he was stealing his half-brother's wife, he wouldn't have seduced Joan, he couldn't be such a rat. He wouldn't bother, women were neither here nor there to him. But then she told herself, that's exactly what he would do. He'd do it as a kind of challenge, and he'd enjoy his little secret until one day, when he was bored with her, he'd tell Joan and blow her world apart.

No, she thought, if he'd known, he'd never have tried to back off. Neil would've made sure that Joan was totally committed to him, just for laughs. Then he'd drop his bombshell. That was the way Neil was. He'd see it as a challenge,

'I'm sure Neil didn't know before,' she said to Jeff. 'Does he know what his mother's saying now?'

'That's a point,' Jeff said. 'I'd better check on that before I write the story. Where did I leave my bag?'

'What bag?'

'I'll need to get this on tape. No one's going to believe it. Maybe I can sell this to the radio.'

It was suddenly as though he hadn't noticed that Sarah was there. She had become a tool of his trade. 'Your office is closed,' he said, almost accusing her, 'where do you think he'll be?'

'Try the hospital, at his sick mother's bedside,' Sarah said with heavy sarcasm. 'Or perhaps the morgue, officially identifying his mistress's body. Or at home, cooking himself a tasty little supper. I'm sure your nurse friend will get you the address.'

Jeff didn't notice the sarcasm.

'Thanks, Babe,' he said, and Sarah heard the front door slam as he ran out of the house.

She listened as, a moment later, he revved the engine of his motorbike and roared off up the street. I bet he did a wheelie, she told herself, and smiled.

And then she thought, what do you think you're smiling at? How's this going to help Angus? If those cops find out about what Neil's mother's saying, they'll probably find some excuse for accusing Angus of killing Joan in a fit of insane jealousy because she ran away with his kid brother.

TWENTY-NINE

Angus breathed a sigh of relief as he closed his front door on Detective Chief Inspector Gifford and his insufferable sidekick Sergeant Knowles. Maybe this time they really hadn't been trying to trick him in some way, maybe they really had come only to inform him about what the woman in the hospital was saying. And they'd told him about Joan almost as an aside, as though he already knew all about it. It was the Carver business they were interested in, but he didn't want to talk to them about the information they'd given him. He didn't want to talk about it to anyone except Sarah. She was the only one who might be able to help him make sense of it.

He told himself, the woman's probably a loony. Maybe seeing me on television triggered some kind of manic maternal delusions. Women quite often propose marriage to serial killers they've seen on TV or in the papers, maybe it was something like that.

And he thought, what was all that about me visiting her at her home yesterday morning? Those cops know I haven't been anywhere, they've had that bloody courting couple watching over me ever since they gave me bail.

He'd actually said exactly that to Gifford when the Chief Inspector asked about an alleged visit to Nellie Carver's house. But then the lumpen Sergeant had jumped in with both feet and said there might have been breaks in the surveillance, they couldn't be sure.

In the end Gifford had sent his sidekick out of the room to check something on the car radio. Gifford had then poured Angus a whisky out of Angus's own bottle and helped himself, too. Angus was surprised, but for some reason he didn't take offence. In the context, it seemed to him not rude, but an appeasing gesture.

Gifford said, 'It would help me a lot if you could tell me

whether it's possible Nellie Carver is telling the truth. I'm not trying to be intrusive, but there are implications if she is . . .'

Angus, his mind on other things, did not take in what he was saying.

'I'm adopted,' he said, 'is that what you're getting at.'

'Are your adoptive parents alive? We could ask them . . .'

'No,' Angus said. 'They're both dead. My father mentioned something once. He said I'd been abandoned and taken to an orphanage and that's where he and my mother found me and chose me to be their son.'

'Any papers?'

'I suppose so. I burned the lot after his death, all his papers. No, I didn't look at them before I set fire to them, because I didn't want to know. As far as I was concerned, they'd been the best possible parents to me and I loved them. I didn't want anything to come between us, like a picture of a birth mother and that sort of thing. I didn't want complications.'

'So it is possible?'

'That Neil Carver is my brother? Hardly.' Then he added, 'God, I hope not.'

Sergeant Knowles came back into the room and Inspector Gifford got up to go. He put his half-empty whisky glass on the sideboard.

'Thank you for the drink, Mr Dillon,' he said. 'We'll keep you posted if there are any further developments.'

'You could try the newspaper archives,' Angus said. 'I was always told I was born in this area. In my experience as a journalist, finding an abandoned baby is usually front page news in the local paper. It's always worth a picture, anyway. That might give you a few facts to go on.'

Gifford nodded. 'I'll put someone on it. It's worth a try.'

'For what it's worth, I thought Carver was born and brought up in New Zealand,' Angus said.

'We'll have to check that out, too,' Gifford said.

When the policemen had gone, Angus went back to the sitting room and wondered what he should do now.

Sarah, he thought, I should talk to Sarah.

But when he tried to phone her number, there was no reply.

Angus lit a cigarette and swallowed the rest of his whisky.

Suddenly he jumped to his feet and stubbed out the cigarette. He knew exactly what he had to do. And he had to do it before he talked to Sarah.

At the hospital he asked for Nellie Carver.

'And you are?' a nurse asked him when he reached the ward.

'Her son,' Angus said. It was easier than trying to explain.

The girl wasn't interested, she had fulfilled the formalities. She pointed down the ward without looking up. 'She's at the end on the right,' she said, 'near the window.'

The place seemed to Angus like an aircraft hangar, an endless line of identical mechanical-looking beds each with a human head protruding from a pillow cockpit. My God, he thought, I've no idea what she looks like, how am I going to know which one is her?

Out of earshot of the nurses, he said, 'Nellie Carver?'

It seemed to him that everyone at the end of the ward was looking at him and recognizing him as the man guilty of killing local children. Of course, he told himself, they're a captive audience, they'll have seen the television. The hostility felt tangible.

Angus was about to turn and run, when he saw a woman with long grey hair hanging loose round an emaciated white face staring at him with a puzzled expression in her sunken blue eyes.

He knew her at once. Not as Nellie Carver. As the woman who had given birth to him. He could not mistake himself in her bony skull and the sad eyes.

Angus felt as though someone had kicked a hole in his stomach and all his organs were draining out on to the shiny scrubbed hospital floor.

He grabbed the rail at the end of her bed to stop himself falling.

'Are you Nellie Carver?' he managed to say.

'Who are you?' she asked. 'What do you want?'

He took her hand. It felt like a bundle of dried twigs wrapped in brittle waxed paper.

'I'm Angus Dillon' he said, and his voice sounded

hoarse. 'I think I might be your son Angus.'

'No,' Nellie said, 'you're not my son Angus. Angus came to see me at home, before they dragged me in here. You're not Angus. Where's Neil? What have you done with Neil?'

Angus moved along the bed to be closer to her. 'Please,' he said, trying to keep his voice down so that the patients in the neighbouring beds could not hear what he was saying. 'Look at me. Really look at me. We look alike. I recognized you at once.'

The deepset, dull blue eyes met his. He saw recognition flare in her eyes, but then it was as though the light went out. He realized that she was blinded by tears. She put up a feeble hand to trace the outline of his face. 'You are, aren't you?' she whispered. 'But you look so ill. You didn't look ill when you last came to see me. When was that?'

'We haven't seen each other before,' he said.

'You came to see me. You can't have forgotten.'

'It must've been Neil,' he said. 'You must've made a mistake. Neil's your son.'

Angus saw the look on her face and added quickly, 'Too.'

'I've been confused,' Nellie said.

'Who is Neil?' Angus asked. 'Is he your stepson, something like that?'

Nellie's mind was wandering. 'Neil was there,' she said, 'he was giving me my medication, but he hasn't been here yet.' She smiled through the tears. 'He knows he has a brother,' she said. 'I told him about you when I saw you on the television, about how I had to leave you and run away with him.'

A nurse appeared at the bedside, bracing and detached. 'Nellie,' the nurse said in a voice like an east wind, 'this is your lucky day. Look who's come to visit you, it's your daughter-in-law.'

Before Nellie could speak, Sarah pushed her way to face Angus across the bed.

'I had to say that,' she whispered fiercely, 'don't give me away or they'll throw me out.'

'Not too long today,' the nurse said, 'we've been quite poorly, haven't we, Nellie?'

Nellie appealed to Angus. 'Who is this woman?' she asked.

The nurse was standing at the end of the bed, looking with clinical approval at the family gathering.

Angus glanced at the nurse.

'This is Sarah,' Angus said to Nellie. 'You can't have forgotten Sarah, she's Neil's wife. Sarah, what do you think of your mother-in-law, letting herself get in such a state?'

He saw Sarah flinch. He thought, she thinks that was cruel, she wanted me to say she was *my* wife. But I can't.

He said, 'Neil couldn't come, so he sent Sarah to see how you are.' If she sees that Nellie believes that, she may forgive me, he told himself.

The nurse turned away to go to another patient. 'Say goodbye to Nellie now,' she said. 'We're about to serve supper. Come back tomorrow, her head will be quite clear by then.'

'But it's only five o'clock,' Sarah said.

'Visiting hours are over,' the nurse said. She would brook no argument.

Nellie suddenly started to laugh. Angus and Sarah were surprised and turned to her.

'I can't believe it,' Nellie said, gasping a little to get the words out, 'Neil's such a big strapping boy and you're so thin.'

The effort of laughing had tired her, and they watched her eyes cloud over as she drifted back into sleep.

Angus suddenly went so white that Sarah thought he was having some sort of seizure.

'My God,' he said, 'I need a drink. I've got to get out of here. Now.'

He turned to walk quickly down the long line of beds to the ward entrance.

'Angus, what is it?' she asked, almost running as she tried to keep up with him.

Once out of the ward, he turned to face her. Although they were still in a No Smoking zone, he took out his packet of cigarettes and put one in his mouth. His hands were shaking so much that he didn't try to light it.

'My God,' he said, 'is this really happening to me? Do you believe what she's saying?'

'I don't know,' Sarah said, 'but she does.'

THIRTY

Later that night, in the third bar Sarah looked into searching for Angus, she saw him sitting on a stool crunched over the counter.

The sight of him gave her a shock; it was as though she had walked in and seen him here before in exactly the same attitude, with the same aura of quiet desperation weighing down his bowed shoulders.

And then she recognized the bar. It was the same one where only a few weeks ago she had come in for a drink after work. That was the night she'd been going to meet Neil, they were going to have dinner together, but he'd texted to say he couldn't make it. Joan Dillon had been sitting at the bar looking like a stunt double of Angus now. It was the way they sat hunched over their drinks, the way they fingered their empty glasses, and clutched the full ones as though they expected the barman to take them back. Sarah thought, they really were a married couple, the way dogs and their owners get to look alike; Angus and Joan must once have been really close to take on each other's physical quirks like that.

Sarah felt her eyes sting as she held back tears. She hesitated, then took a deep breath, went to the bar and drew up a stool for herself beside Angus. He made no sign that he had noticed her coming.

She signalled to the barman to give her whatever Angus was having and to refill his glass at the same time.

'Aren't you going to offer me a cigarette?' she said. 'You usually do at times of crisis.'

He pushed his pack towards her. She didn't take one. She felt a chill of concern because between them this seemed such an unnatural gesture, so unlike other times. It made her feel they were strangers. It's as though he thinks I'm some whore trying to pick him up, she thought, and he wants me to go away.

She pushed the cigarettes back to him and said gently, 'Angus, you can run away from me but sooner rather than later you're going to have to face what's happened.'

For a moment she thought he hadn't heard her. He took no more notice of her than he had when he'd turned away from her outside the ward in the hospital and fled from her.

Then slowly he took another drink and shook his head. 'No,' he said, 'I can't, not now. I can't take it in.'

'Neil's your brother. That's what she said.'

'I don't believe it. We don't look alike.'

'Yes,' she said, 'you do. Now I know, I can't believe I didn't see it. You look like the same person dressed up in different disguises. Except you look much older.'

'No,' he said.

She noticed that his knuckles were white where he gripped his glass. 'It's monstrous,' he said, 'monstrous. Two perfect strangers and suddenly they're my close relatives. Even if that old woman can prove what she says, I don't want to have anything to do with her. And as for my so-called brother, I loathed him the first time I saw him, even before he robbed me of Joan.'

Sarah didn't know what to say or do. It seemed to her that her actions now would determine the future of her relationship with Angus. Her instincts told her to put her arms round him and tell him how much she loved and wanted him. Her head told her that this might be what he wanted her to do, but she feared that if she did she would be colluding with him in failure to grapple the enormity of Nellie's revelation. She thought, he must face it. If he doesn't, it could destroy him. She looked at him with love and saw him exactly as he was; an inadequate man who did not have it in him to create the energy he'd need to force others to accept the truth that he was innocent. He wants to give up, she thought. So much easier to take the blame for what someone else had done and let the rest of his pointless life wash over him in jail. He loves me, Sarah told herself, he knows I love him, but he's worn out, he's not going to struggle for us. He thinks

I'm better off without him, he's probably trying to set me free in his ghastly passive helpless way.

She made one last effort to rouse Angus into some kind of reaction.

'None of this is your fault,' she said. 'Whatever Nellie did, or Neil, whatever the cops think you did, you are innocent.' She spoke low and urgent so that the barman couldn't hear.

Angus said, 'Jesus, think what it must be like for the old woman, discovering her long-lost son's a murder suspect. And not just murder, child killing at that.'

Sarah shivered at the sound of his laugh then.

Angus raised his head to look at her and she saw that his cheeks were wet with tears.

'Please, Sarah, leave me alone, let me think,' he said. 'I've got to sort things out in my head before I do anything else. I need to be alone.'

Sarah had a sudden vision of the future, of years ahead when they would be together and Angus would never change, meeting every crisis with the same hopeless, help-less, apathy. And with that vision she smiled, seeing herself shouldering the remorseless burden of his ineffectuality.

In spite of the setting in this dingy bar, with windows dusty from the passing traffic and bar-stool covers rubbed shiny by decades of passing trade, among weary workers waiting for trains or putting off facing an evening alone, Sarah recognized this as a defining moment in her life. I'm up for it, she thought, I love him.

'I'm strong enough for both of us,' she said aloud. 'For better or for worse.'

Angus gave no sign of having heard her.

The barman said, 'Another drink?'

'No,' she said, 'I've got to go.'

She took out her purse and jotted down Angus's address on a page of her diary and tore it out. 'Here,' she said, 'this is where my friend lives. When the time comes, call a cab to take him home. Please.'

She handed the man a twenty pound note, and he took that and the piece of paper and put them both in his pocket. He gave Angus a sideways look and Sarah, afraid that he was unsympathetic, added, 'He's had some very bad news.'

The barman nodded. 'I'll do my best,' he said.

Sarah hurried out into the street. As she walked quickly towards the police station, she asked herself, is it bad news? A mother he didn't know he had; a brother, even one he doesn't like?

And then she thought of what she knew of Nellie and of Neil, and she smiled. Well, not all good news, then, she told herself.

At the police station she was taken to a small bare room and asked to wait for Chief Inspector Gifford. In the centre of the room was a small table with four chairs on either side. Sarah shivered, although the room was very hot and airless. It could be a set for any television police drama, she thought, and pulled one of the chairs away from the table to sit down. Suddenly she felt nervous. What am I doing here? she asked herself, what kind of story do I think I've got to tell? No one's going to believe me.

She suddenly felt that she should not have come. Why should she do the cops' job for them? What difference did it make if Angus was related to Neil or whatever, it was a private matter. What had made her feel she had to tell Inspector Gifford about what Nellie was saying? If it mattered, they would find out anyway. It wasn't up to her to tell other people's secrets.

She was on the point of giving up and going home, perhaps coming back tomorrow when she'd worked out what she was going to say, when Sergeant Knowles came into the room.

'Apparently you've got something to tell us?' he said.

Sarah wondered if he was always this rude to potential informants, or was it just her?

'I asked to speak to Chief Inspector Gifford,' she said. 'I wanted to talk to him in person.'

'He's not here,' Knowles said. 'I am. What do you want to tell us?'

'I'm not sure I do,' Sarah said. 'It might be nothing.'

Nellie could be dreaming the whole thing, Sarah thought, this stroppy Sergeant will probably accuse me of wasting police time. It probably has no bearing on what they're doing to Angus, it doesn't have anything to do with what they think he did.

'Have you come to retract that phoney alibi you gave Angus Dillon?' Sergeant Knowles said. She could hear the sneer in his voice. She told herself, he thinks I declared war on him and the forces of law and order when I did that. He's sure I lied about it.

'Of course not,' Sarah said, indignant. 'What gave you that idea?'

'It's just you don't look like that sort of girl,' Knowles said. All at once he sounded almost friendly.

'And what sort of girl is that?' she asked, playing along with him.

'Well, you tell me, the sort that has one night stands with a man she scarcely knows and then lies so her boyfriend doesn't find out.'

Sarah gave him a pitying smile. 'Is that what you think, Sergeant? It seems to me you should get out more and meet some real women.'

Knowles glared at her. 'Well, you must admit it looks suspicious,' he said. 'I happen to know you haven't even spoken to Dillon on the telephone since you contrived to get him out on bail. Let alone visited him to catch up on old times.'

His leer was deliberately offensive.

'I suppose it hasn't occurred to you that we might not want to be overheard and overlooked by your grubby police spies when we get together after what's happened?' she said. 'Anyway, you're probably right, I'm wasting my time here. I'll come back tomorrow and talk to your boss.'

She got up to go and, in a gesture she knew he intended to be mocking, Knowles held the door open for her.

'You do that,' he said, and added in an undertone she was meant to hear, 'You may have a better chance of pulling the wool over the boss's eyes, lady, but you don't fool me.'

Sarah was about to deliver some crushing riposte when her mobile phone rang. By the time she had found it among the assorted contents of her handbag, Sergeant Knowles had gone.

'Where are you?' Jeff's voice asked.

'I'm in the police station being messed about by morons,' she snarled at him, wishing it was Knowles whose ear she had at her mercy.

But Jeff didn't notice.

'Something amazing's happened,' he said. 'I've been to interview Nellie Carver.'

'How did you do that?' she asked. 'How did you get them to let you in?'

Jeff sounded impatient. 'I said I was her youngest son from New Zealand,' he said. 'I reckoned with the way she's been carrying on, one son more or less wouldn't make much difference to them. I've got one hell of a story out of her.'

Then his voice changed. 'My God,' he said, 'you're in the police station? You know about the brother thing and you went to the cops? Oh, please, Sarah, please tell me you didn't tell them anything. Did you?'

'As it happens, no, I didn't. I've got to come back first thing tomorrow.'

'Thank you, God,' Jeff said, and she heard his relief across the airwaves. He went on, 'Tell them anything you want tomorrow, Babe, 'cos my story's the front page lead in tomorrow's paper and this is the biggest scoop of the decade. The sky's the limit.'

'But why? Why should anyone else care, except it's a human interest story with a happy ending?' Sarah hesitated and then added, 'Or not, as the case may be.'

She heard Jeff splutter into the phone. I shouldn't spoil his fun, she thought, but Angus is still in the frame for murder. And then she told herself, as far as Jeff's concerned, I suppose that's what makes it a story.

Jeff sounded exasperated. He said, 'For God's sake, Sarah, why are you being so slow, are you drunk?' He went on in the tone of someone explaining to a child why two and two make four. 'Nellie says she had identical twins. Don't you see? Didn't you ever do basic biology at school? Identical twins have identical DNA. The police evidence against Angus is all based on DNA. Maybe it wasn't Angus who killed those kids; maybe it was the other one.'

'Oh, dear God,' Sarah said. The room seemed to sway around her, and Jeff's voice in her ear sounded suddenly far away and faint. 'I thought you'd be pleased,' she heard him say. 'About your precious Angus.'

THIRTY-ONE

N eil Carver jerked the wheel of Nellie's pick-up and plunged off the narrow road to follow a track down through the forest. The daylight was almost gone and he turned on the truck's headlamps to see where he was going between the trees.

Like a wounded animal seeking sanctuary, Neil felt compelled to find himself a dark place where he could take stock. Only darkness could hide what was happening to him and give him time to think.

The track ahead disappeared, apparently colliding with a blank black wall as he came into a dense plantation of conifer trees. He stopped the pick-up and turned off the engine. Here the floor of the wood was dark, without any sign of vegetation breaking through the pall of pine needles which deadened all sound to an uneasy silence.

Neil turned off the vehicle lights. The darkness took on a different quality of menace then. The impenetrable canopy of the intertwined conifer boughs blotted out any hint of light from the sky, as though he'd been transported to another planet without moon or stars. He heard a faint rustling as the wind moved the trees and he shivered, although he could feel the sweat trickling down his back and making his hands slippery on the driving wheel. The wood seemed suddenly alive with whispers from unseen, unknown, aliens who watched and waited.

Time was paralysed. Neil had no idea how long he sat there, almost afraid to breathe. It might have been minutes; or several hours. He felt as though his ability to think was emerging from a long coma.

Gradually he became aware of where he was. Aware, anyway, that he had no idea what place this was, how he had got there, where he could go from here. And why was he driving Nellie's pick-up? Where was his car? How had he got here?

He stared into the dense blackness all around him, screwing up his eyes, unable to be certain if they were open or shut.

Slowly, it came back to him. He'd gone home after he'd taken Joan somewhere. He wasn't sure where, but he would try to remember in a moment. He'd gone upstairs to find Nellie. There was something he had to do to Nellie. Whatever it was, he was late. She was upset. Had Joan said something to her? He wasn't sure.

But Nellie wasn't there.

He searched but he couldn't find her. She'd been taken by force. The bedclothes had been ripped off the bed, and her things on the bedside table were mostly on the floor.

Neil tried to remember who might have taken her. He knew there was someone she'd been afraid of. She'd told Joan, she'd told Joan and that was why Joan had made him take her wherever they'd gone. But it couldn't have been Joan who took Nellie; there was some reason why Joan couldn't do that, he was sure of that.

Where was he now? And why had he come here? He felt as though his brain had fallen into a black pit inside his skull and couldn't climb back into its usual place. His head hurt.

Somewhere in the shadows an owl hooted. Neil jumped, then strained his eyes to see into the darkness. Birds scared him, he was afraid of the silence of their flight. Without meaning to, he sucked in air and it sounded in his ears like a clap of thunder.

Then suddenly his head seemed to clear.

It was Angus who had come for Nellie.

And now he's come for me, Neil thought. He's here, he's found me, he wants to destroy me.

It seemed to Neil that Angus was sitting behind the driving wheel in the pick-up; Angus, not him. Neil knew beyond any question that Angus hated him, that Angus had trapped him, he'd brought him here to frame him for the terrible things that Angus himself had done. How could you? Neil asked Angus, how could you hurt those children?

And yet his heart ached for Angus, because he understood the love he must feel for those poor damaged girls, and he knew that all Angus wanted was the chance to explain. There's no explanation, though, Neil thought, there can be no forgiveness for what Angus did.

There was that poor child, Julie Makepeace, Sarah's brother's child. Angus had killed her. Even the police suspected him, but they hadn't made it stick. So there were the others, the young girls who hadn't been able to fight back, who'd driven him mad with their fiendish, pushy innocence.

Neil felt hot tears coursing down his cheeks. He sobbed Nellie's name over and over again, gasping out the words. 'Why didn't you forget him?' he asked, 'I loved you, we were happy, we never needed him. Why wasn't it enough that we had each other?'

He wept for some time, the muffled sobs echoing amongst the trees.

Then suddenly, he was alert. He blew his nose loudly and heard a sharp clap of wings as a large bird somewhere nearby took off clumsily in alarm. He remembered everything.

He asked himself, is Nellie dead?

He'd fled from the empty house. He'd taken Nellie's pick-up, some instinct telling him it could carry him into a deeper, darker place than his own flash roadster. The police would find his car at the house, they'd know he'd been home. He asked himself, are they looking for me? And if they are, what for? Do they want to tell me that Nellie's dead? I'm next of kin, not Angus.

But perhaps she isn't dead, he thought, perhaps she's going to come out of her drugged confusion and remember. She'll tell them about the medication I gave her, and how I locked her in; they'll find the phenobarbital.

So what? he asked himself. They'll think I gave them to her to help her sleep, that's all. They were given to me as sleeping pills, no one's got any reason to question what I was doing. Is it my fault if she starves herself?

Then he thought, but Angus and I are twins. She'll tell

them that. They'll take my DNA, they'll check. I'll be a suspect as well as Angus.

Come on, he told himself, there's a way out of this. Think of something.

All at once Neil felt that he must escape from the conifer plantation and the secret, sinister woods. He craved bright lights and cheap music and traffic and unsteady drunks in the street. He was Neil, he was in the driving seat, he was in charge. Angus was gone, vanished among the straight regiments of conifer trunks into outer darkness. Angus was still the guilty man, not him.

Neil put the pickup into reverse and barged his way back on to the track. Then he revved the engine and shot forward through the woods, the vehicle lunging across the ruts and sudden gulleys.

Once on the tarmac road, he leaned back in the car seat and relaxed.

It was just before dawn. A gash of bright clear greenish light opened up in the sky above the horizon. The first bright red rays of the sun looked like blood as they appeared. Neil laughed. He had escaped the dark. Daylight was his friend.

It's so beautiful, he thought, life is beautiful. Only Nellie can mess things up.

He told himself, Nellie won't make sense for hours yet. She won't even work things out for herself. No one's going to take much notice of her waffling. I've got time.

He felt sad, but excited, too. It was like a game, a game he knew he was going to win. I can't lose, he thought, I'm bound to win because I'm much cleverer than any of them. They don't even know the game's on.

Nellie would keep. Time enough to deal with her when she was back at home. But first, he told himself, and smiled, I've got to make the opening move.

A few hours later, at about nine o'clock, Neil Carver parked his sports car in the street outside Hunsteignton police station, made a point of locking it, and walked through the revolving door into the building.

THIRTY-TWO

E arly that morning, as Sergeant Knowles made his way slowly along the corridor to Detective Chief Inspector Gifford's office, he heard his boss's voice bellowing his name. Knowles recognized that particular note in Gifford's voice and he knew he was in trouble.

Two young female detective constables smiled at him as they passed him, and one said, 'Cheer up, Sarge, it may never happen.'

Knowles glared at her, saying nothing. He could hear the two girls giggling as they hurried away.

Why's he blaming me? Sergeant Knowles asked himself. It's not my fault.

Knowles didn't really know who to blame, but if he'd happened to meet that creep of a reporter Jeff Acres, or his gabby tart with her weakness for lost causes like Angus Dillon, or Nellie Carver, or her bloody son Neil, he knew he'd be hard put not to arrest them on the spot and find a reason afterwards. He could actually feel himself salivate at the thought of what he'd do to Angus Dillon if he got even half a chance.

Knowles reached the blue door marked with Detective Chief Inspector Gifford's name. He couldn't put it off any longer. He took a deep breath, knocked briefly, and marched into his boss's office.

Gifford slammed the newspaper down on his desk.

'Have you seen this?' he said.

'Yes, sir.'

'How did this happen? How did that reporter get hold of this and we knew nothing about it?'

Knowles thought, does he know Angus Dillon's whore came in last night and this must be what she wanted to tell us? He can't know. No one in CID knew she was here. And if he doesn't know, I'm not going to tell him.

He said, 'If you ask me, Sir, this is some sort of stunt
Angus Dillon's pulling with Jeff Acres to get himself off
the hook. He was a journalist, wasn't he? Those kind of
people stick together. Don't Acres's and Dillon's squeeze
share a house? Dillon's sure to have told her and she's told
her tame reporter.'

Gifford grunted, a concession, Knowles knew, that his
boss saw his point and that he was off the hook for now.

'This blows our case apart,' Gifford said. 'Get uniform
to pick up Neil Carver.'

Sergeant Knowles hesitated. 'And Dillon?' he asked.

'First things first, Sergeant,' Gifford said. 'Lets get
Carver's DNA tested first. If it doesn't match Dillon's,
we've got that grubby journalist Jeff Acres and his sleazy
rag cold.'

Knowles didn't dare ask, 'What if it does?'

'What if he doesn't want to cooperate? Neil Carver, I
mean,' he said.

'Arrest the bugger,' Gifford roared at him. 'Arrest him
for anything you can think of, we can always say sorry later
if we have to.'

Knowles turned to go. He couldn't help looking relieved
that Gifford hadn't found out about Sarah Makepeace's visit
last night, but he knew Gifford well and he sensed that his
boss suspected that he was hiding something.

'What's going on—?' Gifford started to say, and then the
telephone rang.

Gifford answered it. 'Yes?' he snapped.

Knowles tried to hear what the caller was saying but he
couldn't. Then Gifford slammed the receiver down on its
rest.

'Don't bother bringing Neil Carver in,' he said. 'He's
here. He's downstairs waiting to talk to us.'

THIRTY-THREE

S arah overslept that morning. She'd spent most of the night unable to sleep, thinking of Angus. Every time she closed her eyes she'd remembered the way Angus had looked when she left him in the bar, defeated and hopeless. She worried that the barman hadn't bothered to call him a taxi and simply turned him out into the night. Even if Angus had been sober, the way he looked would have been an invitation to every mugger in town.

Then, as dawn broke, she fell asleep and dreamed of him. A disturbing dream in which she went into the bar where she had left him and found that he had taken root there and couldn't escape. He pleaded with her to help him, but when she took up a knife and tried to sever the roots, he screamed in pain, and his blood began to flow across the floor.

She felt shaky as she went to the kitchen to make coffee. Please, she thought, let Jeff have gone to work. I don't want to talk to him now.

But Jeff was sitting at the kitchen table with the newspaper spread out in front of him. He wasn't just reading his front page story, his eyes seemed to devour it; he even repeatedly licked his lips at the sweet taste of success.

'Here,' he said, 'have you seen this? This is the best thing I've ever done.'

Sarah understood what this story meant to him. She knew that he now saw his way clear to fame and fortune. But she was repelled by the gloating look on his face.

And she was grumpy from lack of sleep. 'I'll look at it later,' she said.

'It's got a terrific show,' Jeff said.

'I don't see what you've got to be so pleased about,' Sarah said. 'It's not as though you've done something creative or anything like that. It's other people's stories, you just write down what they tell you.'

Sarah knew she was being deliberately churlish but she couldn't stop herself.

But Jeff didn't seem to mind. He laughed at her and said, 'Hey, Babe, what's up? You're not jealous, are you? Think what it means to you, as well as me. I can walk into one of the nationals now. We can get married and move to London.'

Sarah said, 'No. I don't want to marry you. I don't want to go to London.'

She was horrified at herself. She hadn't meant to say anything, let alone blurt out what was in her mind. It was as though she was under the influence of some sort of truth drug and couldn't stop herself saying what she really felt.

She tried to soften her blunt words.

'Jeff, I'm sorry,' she said, 'I didn't mean it to come out like that.'

He looked at her in amazement.

'But we agreed. You said you'd marry me.'

'You blackmailed me into it by threatening me,' she said.

Jeff looked at her in astonishment. He said, 'What do you mean, you don't want to marry me? Babe, I've got a big future, I'll be able to give you anything you want. You don't know what you're saying.'

The kettle began to boil. Sarah made coffee for both of them.

It's now or never, she told herself.

'Jeff, I don't want to marry you,' she said. 'And I don't think you really want to marry me. We don't want the same things. You've got a chance to break into London now, and we both know you'll be better off on your own. I'd hold you back. You'd soon grow to hate me, and I'd probably hate you, too. You need to be free . . .'

Stop while you're ahead, she told herself, don't go blathering on, he'll think you don't mean it.

Jeff looked at her with his head slightly on one side, as though he was weighing up what she'd said. 'I s'pose it's true,' he said, considering her argument, 'I'd need a hundred per cent commitment, and if you're not ready for that . . .'

The arrogance of the man, she thought, it's as though he's interviewing me for the job of being his wife.

'It's best we realize before it's too late,' she said.

'Why did you have to get involved in this business with Angus Dillon?' he said, and his tone was plaintive. 'You haven't been the same since that dinner party you went to with Neil Carver.' Something suddenly seemed to occur to him. 'Please tell me you're not in love with Neil Carver?' he said.

'Don't be ridiculous,' she said, irritated that he could be so dense. 'Actually, I'm in love with Angus.'

Jeff laughed. 'Now who's being ridiculous?' he said.

Sarah shrugged. 'Suit yourself,' she said. 'But I mean it about us being over. We'll have to sell this place anyway, if you're moving to London. I can't afford to buy you out.'

'Can you organize that?' Jeff said, checking his pockets for the keys to his motorbike and his credit cards. 'Feel free to stay on till you've found something else. It'll take a while to sell anyway, and I'll be busy getting myself fixed up in the Smoke.'

My God, Sarah thought, he's made for the tabloids.

'I'm planning to move out today, actually,' she said. 'There's no point in prolonging the agony, is there? Perhaps you can get your new secretary on the case?'

Sarah asked herself, why are you saying this? What's got into you? Why move out? It's not as though you've anywhere else to go.

'OK,' Jeff said. 'See you later.'

He seemed undecided about whether to shake hands with her or kiss her. Instead he waved and shouted 'Bye' as he left the house.

Sarah felt stunned. She couldn't believe that her relationship with Jeff was over. And so suddenly, so casually. It had gone on for so long and been so close. But not for some time, she thought, I've almost forgotten what it was like then. But the end had been so unemotional, so cool. Sarah felt disappointed at the anticlimax.

She tried to gather her thoughts, decide what to do now.

Talk about throwing the baby out with the bathwater, she thought, now I've got no man, no home, no prospects.

And yet she knew why she had forced this position on herself. For once in your life, Angus, she thought, *do* something about it. You've only got to ask.

But she had no real hope that when he knew how completely she had made herself available to him, he would find the energy to act.

She looked around the familiar kitchen. It had taken her years to get it just as she wanted it. She'd taken such care, choosing the colour of the tiles behind the cooker, picking out the small details which made the place home. She'd never been able completely to get rid of the blood stain on the wall behind the work surface where she'd cut herself dicing carrots. And then there were all the Le Creuset saucepans she'd saved up for from her first six months' pay packets. Jeff would expect his share; the security of having everything as she wanted it would be lost for ever.

Well, she told herself, there's no help for it, I'll have to start again from scratch.

But first she had to know whether she must start again alone, or if there was a chance that Angus could be her fellow traveller.

So, later that morning, she drove to the Dillon cottage. Sock, in a cat box on the back seat, was her excuse. She would ask Angus to take him in until she found a permanent home, for him and for herself.

For once, she could see no sign of the police surveillance team, but she presumed they were there somewhere and waved gaily for their benefit.

Now that she was here, she was nervous of what she would find. He was probably still drunk, passed out somewhere. Or maybe he'd started on the hair of the dog. It seemed to her that her heart was bursting with things she wanted to say to him, and she dreaded the state he'd be in when she found him.

She knocked on the door and there was a long wait before he came to answer it. Oh, God, she thought, he'll be all maudlin and stupid, still half-drunk. She wanted to turn and flee, but her knees felt too weak to carry her.

But then she saw him opening the door and he didn't stink of whisky and try to fumble her in greeting. He had shaved and he was wearing a clean shirt and she wanted to weep in relief.

'Come in,' he said, 'I'm glad you're here. I was putting off ringing in case the cops are listening.'

'I see the surveillance team have moved on.'

'Yes,' he said, 'they went off in a hurry yesterday and they haven't returned.'

There was an awkward silence while they tried to think of something to say.

'What have you got there?' Angus asked at last, pointing at the cat box.

'It's Sock, my cat. Could he stay here with you for a while?'

She didn't explain and Angus didn't ask. They both knew that what they had to talk about was too important to be complicated by small talk about the cat.

'Of course,' Angus said. 'We'll put him in the kitchen to get used to new surroundings.'

She followed him through the house and shut the kitchen door behind her. Angus put a saucer of milk on the floor and Sarah opened the door of the cat box. They both watched in silence as Sock emerged and stalked across the floor with his tail in the air.

At last she asked, 'Are you all right?'

He smiled because he could tell she was surprised that he seemed to be.

'Yes,' he said. 'I'm sorry about last night, I needed to think things through. And I have. We need to talk.'

'Yes,' she said.

'There's so much I want to say to you,' he said, 'but there are things we've got to deal with first. Urgent things. We can't sort anything out and move on until they're sorted. Do you understand?'

'You've seen the paper? About Nellie Carver saying you and Neil are twins, and what that means?'

'That's the first question we've got to deal with,' he said.

'Yes,' she said. 'But where do we start?'

'I've been trying to imagine what I'd do if I were Neil,' he said. 'And I think Nellie's life's in danger.'

'My God,' she said, 'you really think Neil will try to kill her?'

'He's insane,' Angus said, 'he must be insane. Once the police know about the DNA match, he knows he's as much a suspect as me. Nellie is the one person who probably knows something that'll give him away. He's got to make sure she can't tell them anything.'

'But she's safe in hospital?' Sarah said. 'He must know the police will want to talk to him, he won't go there.'

'They're sending her home,' Angus said. 'Now the drugs are out of her system, there's no reason to keep her there.'

'But where will she go?' Sarah said. 'Back home to Heart's-ease House? You mean she'll be there alone with Neil?'

'He hasn't been to the hospital,' Angus said. He grinned at Sarah. 'Just his wife!'

They were in the kitchen, and Angus put the coffee percolator on the stove to reheat. He looked worried.

'I know, I'm sorry,' Sarah said, 'I didn't mean to complicate things when I said that.'

'It could help, actually. No one would think twice about discharging her into the care of her son and her daughter-in-law.'

Sarah said, 'Jeff and I have just split up. Just now. I've told him I'm moving out today.'

She saw the sudden relief on his face, and then doubt.

'Would you move in here?' he asked. 'There's plenty of room. If I brought Nellie here, we could make sure she wasn't left alone.'

'From what I know of hospitals, it takes hours to get people discharged,' she said. 'If you get going now, you can wait for her and bring her here.'

'I left my car at the hospital last night,' Angus said. 'I forgot all about it.'

He looked puzzled, as though he couldn't quite remember what he'd done last night.

Sarah said, 'Take my car and go and pick her up. I'll wait for you here.'

'I don't know what to say,' he said. He took her hand and she could feel that he was shaking.

Then he opened a drawer and took out a long metal key. 'Take this,' he said, 'it's for the front door. They gave it back to me with Joan's things. We'll change the locks as soon as I get round to it, but we must keep the place locked and you'll need to get in. Lock yourself in, too. I'm probably overreacting but better safe than sorry.'

Sarah was startled at the way he seemed to have thought everything out. She was about to say something flippant about how discovering a family he didn't know he had was making a new man of him, but then she saw his expression and realized that he believed they might really be in danger.

She locked the door behind him and then, from the sitting room window, watched him walk down the path to her car. The heavy key and old-fashioned lock on the front door gave her a feeling of security. It would take more than a credit card or a heavy kick to break through that. Anyway, she thought as she watched her car disappear round a bend in the lane, it's grotesque to think of this cottage needing to be defended, it's just not the sort of place where bad things could possibly happen.

It was indeed a classic peaceful English scene; roses scrambled over the fence, almost hiding the deserted lane where overgrown cow parsley and mallow gossiped across the tarmac. Sarah told herself, it's inconceivable that anything as horrible as murder could happen here.

But then, as she watched brown butterflies flitting round a rampant honeysuckle, a sparrow hawk swooped low over the fence from the lane and into a bush near the gate. There was a shriek, then desperate protest as the bird emerged with a screaming chaffinch clutched in its talons. It sped away, and there was a shocked silence before at last subdued hidden birds resumed their chirping.

Suddenly, the overgrown garden and the quiet road was no longer a peaceful idyll. The sun still shone, a gentle breeze still stirred the long grass and the fronds of ferns under the fence, but the tangled thorned roses and the dark shadows of trees seemed threatening now, not peaceful at all, but savage and hostile, protecting from view a sinister place full of menace.

Sarah felt cold. She was uneasy. All at once she was overwhelmed by the thought that this had been Joan's home, and that Joan was dead. It almost seemed, though, that she was still here, invisible in the house, her unhappiness like ingrained damp in the room.

Sarah told herself not to be fanciful, but although it was still only early afternoon, she went round the house turning on lights.

She knew she couldn't expect Angus to return for hours yet. If only I had a car, I wouldn't feel so trapped, she told herself, but it wasn't just that, she was filled with a superstitious terror that from the other side of the locked front door she was being watched by something evil which would show no mercy.

She sat in Angus's chair by the fire in the sitting room to await his return. It was the only way she could think of to feel closer to physical contact with him. But she still felt that she didn't belong here, that the cottage was holding itself aloof.

She began to dread being alone here after dark.

THIRTY-FOUR

Neil Carver made no move to get up from his chair at the table in the interview room when Detective Chief Inspector Gifford and Sergeant Knowles came in.

Instead, he made a show of looking at his watch, as though they were late for an appointment. He was clearly furious at being kept waiting.

'Well, we're here now, Mr Carver, so lets not waste any more of your time,' Gifford said, acknowledging the body language but without apology, pulling out a chair opposite Neil and sitting down. 'What do you want to say to us?'

Sergeant Knowles sat next to Gifford. He took out a pack of cigarettes and offered it to Neil, who shook his head impatiently.

'I came here because I presumed you would want to interview me, in the light of what my mother has apparently been saying,' Neil said. 'I thought I was helping, coming here to make it easy for you.'

He flicked back his fashionably cut, smooth blond hair with an ostentatiously manicured hand. Like a damned girl, Inspector Gifford thought, well aware that Neil Carver was deliberately drawing attention to the contrast with his own thinning head. In retaliation, he put both hands on the table and spread his long, strong fingers, so unlike Neil's chubby little hands.

He said, 'Indeed, Mr Carver, we appreciate your help. But why do you think we're interested in interviewing you?'

'Oh, for God's sake,' Neil said, 'because of the DNA, of course.'

Gifford contrived to make his smile both puzzled and encouraging as he said, 'The DNA?'

Neil was growing red in the face. 'My mother's saying Angus Dillon and I are both her sons, isn't that right?' he said, in the tone of an exasperated man trying to teach basic English to a foreigner.

'I believe this is true,' Gifford said, now looking as though he sympathized with a son saddled with such a fanciful mother. 'We haven't interviewed her yet.'

'She's saying we're twins, isn't she? Identical twins.'

'I believe so,' Gifford said, and smiled again.

'And identical twins have identical DNA, right?'

'Yes,' Gifford said.

Neil was getting irritated at the policeman's attitude.

'Your evidence against Angus Dillon depends on DNA, isn't that right? You'll want to test mine because if it's identical Nellie may be telling the truth and you'll have to consider me as a suspect as well as Dillon, right?'

Gifford studied his fingers on the top of the table with apparent fascination. 'If, as you say, the evidence against Mr Dillon depended on DNA,' he said, 'then we would ask you to provide a sample for testing.'

'Well, here I am, aren't you going to get on with it?' Neil said.

Like a snake suddenly making an attacking strike, Gifford suddenly leaned forward across the table. Knowles, who had been wondering why his boss was being so polite to this obvious attention seeker, actually jumped in surprise.

'But then, Mr Carver, as you are undoubtedly about to tell me, if you and Angus Dillon have identical DNA, we can't pursue a case against either one of you, can we?'

'Why can't we?' Knowles asked the Inspector. 'We'll have both the bastards for the price of one.'

Neil smiled at Knowles, but he spoke to Gifford, 'That is what I came to say, basically,' he said. Then he turned to Knowles: 'I'm afraid it means you can't make a case stick against either one of us because it could always have been the other.'

Gifford leaned back in his chair and stretched his legs under the table. He kicked Neil as he did so, and said quickly, 'I'm so sorry, was that your foot?'

'You can't hold either of us, can you? You'll have to start the case again from scratch.'

'Please don't imagine that we won't do that,' he said. 'DNA isn't the only way we can make a murder charge stick, as I'm sure you're well aware, Mr Carver.'

Gifford got up and walked towards the door. 'Since you're here, I'll get someone to take you to have a sample taken,' he said. He opened the door and called to a constable in the corridor outside.

'Good luck to you,' Neil said. 'I can only say how sorry I am that this er . . . development means that a serial child-killer will go free.'

Gifford was talking to the constable in the doorway.

'Not if I get my hands on him, he won't,' Knowles muttered.

Neil smiled at him, showing his perfect capped teeth which, under the harsh unshaded overhead light looked a slightly less than perfect white.

'The law's the law of course, but I don't like to think what the press will make of this if there's another kiddie killed,' he said. Then he seemed to be struck with an idea. 'Of course, Nellie may be lying,' he said. 'Old women get funny ideas in their heads sometimes, particularly if they're taking strong drugs.'

'You mean we could get Dillon in and force him to confess before the DNA thing comes out?' Sergeant Knowles said. 'So far it's only in the local paper. We'd have to have a confession, though, it's the only way now. Time's getting tight.'

'Well, I know what I'd do,' Neil said. 'Killing and sexually abusing children is unforgivable, you have to be prepared to bend the rules to stop it happening again. That's what I think, anyway.'

'That's true,' Knowles said.

'What's true?' Inspector Gifford said, coming back to the table.

Neil got up, looking at his watch. 'Look, Chief Inspector, I'm sorry, this has all taken so long I can't wait now. I'm already late for an important site meeting with a client. I'll come back tomorrow for the DNA test.'

'It won't take long,' Gifford said.

'Look, I came here voluntarily and I don't think you can keep me here against my will. If Nellie's not making it up, we know what the results will be, I don't see that a few hours will make much difference.'

Neil winked at Knowles, who pretended not to notice.

'No time like the present, Mr Carver,' Gifford said.

'I've told you, I haven't time now,' Neil insisted. 'I came here to help, but you kept me waiting for ages and I don't think you have the right to stop me leaving. If you have, I'll call my solicitor and refuse to give a sample, and that will all take much longer because I don't think you've grounds to force me to do anything until you've checked out Nellie's story. That will all take a lot longer than if you and I agree a time tomorrow.'

Gifford decided not to argue. He was acutely aware of how his bosses would react to the expense of a legal battle if Neil Carver decided to refuse to give a sample. 'We need to speak to Mrs Carver,' Gifford said. 'I understand she's leaving hospital today, and that she's going to stay with Angus Dillon. Apparently she's agreed to that. We don't want her to feel any pressure, so we'll see her there first thing tomorrow. The doctor says she's clearer in the head early in the morning. Perhaps you'd come in then, Mr Carver? I'll tell the desk sergeant you're coming. And thank you for your cooperation.'

Neil went to the door and opened it. 'Till tomorrow, then,' he said. He smiled at Knowles, then went out and shut the door behind him.

Gifford frowned. 'What's been going on between you two?' he asked.

Knowles picked up his packet of cigarettes from the table and put them in his pocket. 'Going on, Sir? I don't know what you mean,' he said.

'You watch your step, Sergeant,' Gifford told him, 'don't you go doing anything behind my back. There have been far too many cock ups already on this case.'

'Is he right?' Knowles asked. 'If he's got the same DNA as Dillon, does that mean we can't get that bastard?'

'It means we have to find more evidence to fix Dillon

as our killer,' Gifford said. 'Or, of course, to make a case against Neil Carver. Maybe he's our man.'

'That's not very likely, though, is it? He came in here of his own free will, and he's as keen to nail the bastard as any of us. Anyway, he's not the type, is he?'

'You mean he looks rich and well-dressed and keeps his nails clean? Don't be fooled by appearances, Knowles, murderers don't look like killers, whatever the public may think after seeing the photographs of suspects they print in the press. It would make our job a lot easier if they did.'

THIRTY-FIVE

It was after midnight. Nellie had long since gone up to bed. She was still weak, and it had taken more than an hour for her to tell Angus all that she wanted to say to him about what had happened at the time of his birth. And then Angus had had to tell her about the couple who had adopted him, about his childhood, and what had happened to the people he called Mum and Dad.

They were both exhausted by the end. So was Sarah from sitting listening to them. Nellie and Angus were strangers, but there was so much emotion pent up between them, so much neither dared to say to the other. Angus didn't even call Nellie by her name. He had before, in the hospital, but now he felt inhibited by the fact that she was his mother and he couldn't call her Mum. Even to call her Nellie seemed over familiar. It seemed to establish a relationship that did not yet exist. Angus felt that she was a stranger and he was waiting for her to be formally introduced.

Nellie was still confused after the days she'd spent under sedation without food or drink, but her mind was much clearer than it had been in the hospital. She was very shy of Angus. She felt she couldn't ask him questions about what had happened to him after she abandoned him, or about the people who had loved him. She thought that he must hate her for what she'd done. And, if he could find it in his heart to understand why she had had to leave him, she knew she could never explain herself why she had chosen Neil over him when she had to make that decision.

Earlier in the evening, Angus had lighted a fire in the inglenook in the sitting room. In spite of the season, he and Sarah had felt inexplicably cold when they returned to the house, a sort of inner cold that had nothing to do with the temperature outside.

Angus was sitting in his chair beside the embers when Sarah came down from checking on Nellie.

'Thank you,' he said, drawing deep on his cigarette before throwing the stub into the fireplace. 'If she and I can really forge some sort of relationship, it'll be down to you being here tonight.'

'You make me feel like a kind of referee,' Sarah said. 'You'd have found a way to talk without me here.'

'No,' Angus said, 'I don't think so. She and I are alike, we clam up and leave everything unsaid. To be honest, that's the main reason I believe she may really be my birth mother. God, I hate that phrase, it's so manipulative. Did you notice she never mentioned Neil except in passing?'

Sarah stretched out opposite him in the chair she supposed must have once been Joan's. 'I actually felt sorry for him,' she said softly. 'I think she's always taken out the guilt she felt about you on him. He wanted her love more than anything, and she's always withheld it and never let herself love him as a way of punishing herself for what she did to you.'

Angus yawned. 'It's no good,' he said, 'I can't even think about Neil tonight. I'm too tired to think about anything. I can't even decide if there really was any reason to think Nellie was in danger.'

'It doesn't matter now, she's safe here. We'll face it all in the morning, everything will be clearer then.'

They sat in silence for a while, listening to the faint crackling of the dying fire. Somewhere outside an owl started hooting, and then broke off when, close by, a vixen voiced her weird and savage cry, the primitive voice of the wild animal in the lonely night.

Sarah started awake suddenly. She didn't know what had suddenly put her on the alert. Angus was asleep in his chair. As she looked at his thin face relaxed in sleep, she told herself, it's the first time I've ever seen him look at peace.

A log had shifted in the fire, and there was a spurt of flame among the ashes. That must have been it, she told herself, there was nothing else, unless it was that chilling call of the predatory fox outside.

Still feeling a bit fuzzy, she started upstairs to check on Nellie.

My God, she thought, it's freezing away from the fire. Nellie must have opened her window. She's probably the old school, can't sleep without a bloody gale blowing in.

Well not tonight, Sarah said to herself, tonight this cottage is going to be hermetically sealed before we go to bed.

She listened for a moment at Nellie's door. She could hear the old woman's heavy breathing inside, as she had the last time she checked. Very carefully so as not to wake her, Sarah opened the door and slipped into the room, closing the latch behind her.

There was a moon outside and Sarah could see the curtain moving against the light of the window. The wind must've got up, she hadn't noticed a breath of air before.

She started to make her way towards the open window, feeling for the end of the bed so as not to knock against it and wake Nellie.

Sarah was a few feet from the bed. Suddenly a huge dark shadow reared up between her and the window, a human shape with arms raised.

'Nellie?' she gasped.

But she was not quick enough. She found herself gripped in an embrace which jerked the breath out of her. There was something soft across her face. She struggled but could not push it away. She felt the pinch of cold hard fingers tightening round her throat.

She forced herself to go limp and felt the grip on her throat relax a little. He thinks he's killed me, she told herself.

She noticed the silence, and thought how unnatural it was to be aware of such a thing. And then she thought, he's killed Nellie.

Sarah held her breath and knew that if she was quick she had a chance to escape the crippling grasp of her assailant. Then, suddenly, she struck out with all her might, and hit him in the Adam's apple with the edge of her flattened hand.

He staggered backwards towards the window, making a

hoarse kind of groaning in his throat. Sarah stepped towards him, bringing her knee up into his groin with all her force, then linked her fingers and brought her hands down like a hammer on the back of his neck as he doubled up.

He roared in pain and, on his knees, lunged towards her. She turned and ran for the door, but he caught her ankle and brought her down before she could reach it. She managed to turn on her back so she could kick him, then his weight was on top of her, pressing her against the bare floorboards.

He grabbed a clump of her hair and began to thump her head on the floor. She tried to scream, scratching at his hands in her hair. His wrist was against her cheek and she managed to grab the flesh in her teeth and bite as hard as she could. He started back with a snarl, his arm raised to hit her.

And then he was jerked backwards away from her, his body contorted as though in a sudden cramp, before he toppled sideways and lay still.

Sarah waited, not trying to move until the breath came back into her body. Her body felt as though it had been vacuum packed and someone had just let in the air. She was struggling to her knees when light flooded the room.

Angus, staring in disbelief at the brass poker in his hand, was standing beside Neil.

'I think I've killed him,' he said.

Sarah felt Neil's neck for a pulse. 'He's not dead,' she said. 'You saved my life. He was trying to kill me.'

She got unsteadily to her feet, suddenly dizzy. 'Quick,' she said, 'I think he may have killed Nellie. He was throttling her when I came in.'

Nellie was lying on her back in bed, her eyes staring. Sarah gagged, sure that she was dead.

But then Nellie said in a hoarse, weak voice, 'Neil tried to kill me. My own son. I'm his mother, why would he want to kill me?'

Angus took her hand. He said gently, 'He's sick, he doesn't know what he's doing.'

Aside to Sarah, he said, 'Are you all right? Can you call an ambulance?'

As Nellie made an effort to sit up, the dark red marks around her throat were exposed.

'I'm calling the police,' Sarah said to Angus. 'You find something to tie Neil up. We don't want him to come to and have another go.'

But before she could reach the bedroom door on her way downstairs to telephone, there was a pounding on the stairs and Sergeant Knowles burst into the room, followed by two uniformed constables.

Knowles glanced around the room, taking in Neil lying unconscious on the floor and the lurid marks on Nellie's neck.

He leapt at Angus, pinning his arms behind his back.

'I've got you now, you bastard,' he said. 'What's been happening here?' No one could mistake his gloating tone. He had been proved right; he had proved Gifford wrong, and he had saved Neil Carver's mother's life. Best of all, he had cut a swathe through all that nonsense about inadequate evidence and caught his killer in the act.

'My son tried to kill me,' Nellie quavering voice confirmed Knowles's triumph.

One of the constables handcuffed Angus as the Sergeant gripped his arms. Then Knowles released his grip.

'I came here to bring you in for more questioning,' Knowles said to Angus, 'but I've got you bang to rights now. By dawn you'll be begging me to let you take the blame for every unsolved child-killing on the books anywhere in the country.'

'No!' Sarah cried, trying to push Knowles away from Angus.

Suddenly, Nellie's voice rang out with a power none of them had ever heard from her before.

'Not him, you fool. My son Neil tried to kill me, not Angus.'

Knowles shouted at her. 'But you said he tried to kill you. You said Angus Dillon is your son.'

'He is,' Nellie said, very calm. 'He saved my life. He saved Sarah's life. Neil attacked her when she came in and stopped him killing me.'

Knowles looked down at Neil. There was blood on the side of his head where Angus had hit him, but he was beginning to come to. They could hear him moan.

The Sergeant shrugged and jerked his head at one of the constables, who stepped forward and unlocked the handcuffs on Angus.

'Why were you carrying the poker when you came into the room?' Knowles said. 'You were intending to strike your mother dead, weren't you?'

'I heard Sarah shout,' Angus said, 'I grabbed the first thing to hand and rushed upstairs to help.'

Knowles said nothing. One of the constables was calling for an ambulance on his mobile phone.

Knowles thought, God help me, the Chief Inspector's going to go berserk when he finds out I took it on myself to come here to take Dillon in and give him the treatment to make him confess.

The Sergeant looked at Nellie and then at Neil. Perhaps not, he told himself, he can't say much. I've saved Nellie Carver's life, and the girl's. I've caught the killer, after all. I've got a result, which he wouldn't have. The old woman will testify, and the tart. Thanks to me, we've got indisputable evidence now. Even Charlie Gifford can't take that away from me.

THIRTY-SIX

Neil was sitting cross-legged on the bed in his cell staring, Buddha-like, at the door. He didn't move as Angus came in and walked across the cell to sit beside him on the bed. The custody sergeant left them together and went out, slamming the metal door shut behind him.

For several minutes neither Neil nor Angus spoke. Then Neil said, 'So you came. I didn't think you would.'

Angus sat on the edge of the bed, as far away from Neil as space allowed. He could not help himself staring at this virtual stranger, who could apparently claim to be more like him than any other human being.

He thought, I never liked him. He disgusts me.

He gazed at Neil, seeking, and at the same time dreading, even the faintest resemblance to himself.

'I didn't think I would either,' Angus said. 'I don't know why I'm here.'

At least speaking aloud stopped the fearful train of thought that he and this human freak of nature could be identical halves of a single man.

Instinctively, Angus resorted to the journalistic experience which had shielded him emotionally, like protective clothing in the face of all kinds of extreme human behaviour. He was amazed, and also sickened, at his own ability not to be involved with the creature dressed in some sort of paper boiler suit sitting beside him on the bench in the grubby white-walled cell.

'Have you seen Nellie?' Neil asked.

Angus shook his head. He was repelled by a note of eagerness in Neil's voice. He sounds as though he thinks Nellie will come to his rescue, Angus thought; as though he thinks she owes him something.

He couldn't stop himself gazing at Neil, his eyes moving

from feature to feature, trying to find a connection with himself. Then he caught Neil's eyes examining him in the same way. They both looked away and stared fixedly at the wall.

There was another long silence. Angus coughed and Neil said, 'It's funny, isn't it, with everything that's happened between us, and there's nothing to say?'

'There's too much to say,' Angus said. 'It's probably better not to start. We're much further apart even than total strangers.'

Neil said, 'If it would help to shout at me and tell me how much you hate me, go ahead. Or you could beat me up. I'm sure that's what that cop wants, because then he can knock the shit out of me and blame you.'

Angus said, 'I couldn't bring myself to touch you.'

'If I'd known we were brothers,' Neil said, 'things might've been different. About Joan . . .'

Angus found it hard to believe what he was hearing.

'This has nothing to do with Joan,' he said. 'It's not even that you tried to make me guilty of your crimes. It's what happened to those young girls.'

'That's not my fault,' Neil said. He spoke with complete conviction, like a child denying blame.

'You're insane,' Angus said. 'Surely you know that?'

'So it's not my fault, is it? You can't blame me, can you? Not if I'm sick.' Neil uncrossed his legs and turned to look at Angus.

Angus shivered. Perhaps we're not so different, he thought, I never took responsibility for anything.

They were both silent again. This is awful, Angus thought, we're like two people acting out an overwritten scene in a bad play. He asked, 'Why did you ask me to come?'

Neil looked away. Angus had to lean forward to hear what he was saying.

'I don't really know,' he said. 'I suppose I wanted to look into your eyes and see myself before—'

Angus was angry. 'Stop that,' he said, 'stop trying to fool yourself and me. There's no connection between us, nothing at all.'

'Oh,' Neil said, 'that may be what you want to believe, but you don't mean it. You can't. Why else would you be here? I'm your brother, your twin brother. You can't just pretend I don't exist.'

Angus smiled. It was the polite but impatient gesture of someone denying acquaintance with a stranger who claimed a previous connection.

'No,' he said, 'I'm not your brother. We may share the same DNA, but that doesn't make you my brother. There's more to brotherhood than that. We don't know each other, and I don't want to know you. I don't like you; I never did. You are nothing to do with me.'

Angus surprised himself with the certainty that what he said was true. He realized that until then he had not really been convinced of his own feelings.

'Don't say that,' Neil said. 'At least tell me you'll try to forgive me.'

'It's nothing to do with me,' Angus said. 'Ask your mother to forgive you, if you dare, not me. I don't feel any connection with you, not as a person. I hate what you did, but I don't care about you.'

Angus stopped. He had spoken partly out of bravado, as a way of setting himself apart from Neil. Now he was astonished to find that he had spoken the truth.

Neil was saying, 'I loved her, she was my Mum and I loved her. But she never loved me, not enough. I was never good enough for her, however hard I tried. Of course I didn't know why. I didn't know she was always thinking she'd picked the wrong son.'

'I don't care about all that,' Angus said. 'It's got nothing to do with me. Perhaps the psychiatrists in prison can help you come to terms with what you've done.'

'I wanted those kids to feel loved and never have to learn the truth. Love betrays everyone. You know that. Look at Joan. I wish I'd been able to die before I knew that. That's what Nellie did to me.'

Angus wanted to shout, 'But now there's Sarah and she will never betray me. Whatever happens, I know Sarah will never betray me.'

He knew that he should get up and go. He had no intention of being sucked into Neil's nightmare. What took him by surprise was that he knew beyond the shadow of a doubt that there was no danger of this happening. He had been worried, when he came here, that long years of apathy had left him defenceless against emotional bullying. He had been afraid that Neil could make him feel guilty that he did not share the evil in his brother. Now he was free.

But he couldn't just get up and leave; it wouldn't be polite. Polite? Angus almost laughed aloud at his own absurdity.

For the first time, he felt some sort of pity for the man who might have been his brother, but wasn't and never could be now. But that pity wasn't for Neil. Neil was not that lost brother.

He asked, 'What happened, Neil?'

'What happened to make me into a monster, you mean?' Neil said. 'You think I'm a monster, don't you?'

'Yes,' Angus said.

The bald word seemed to vibrate in the air between them like metal struck with a hammer.

'I found Julie Makepeace's body,' Angus said. 'You can't expect me to forgive the man who did that.'

'You know,' Neil said, 'afterwards . . . when I'd done those things . . . it was as though I'd always had an evil twin who . . . well, who did terrible things to those beautiful children. It wasn't me, you see, it was him, but we were trapped in the same body, the evil twin and me, and now I get the blame but it was him . . .'

'But why . . .?'

Neil clasped his head in his hands. 'They were so beautiful,' he whispered, as though he couldn't bear to hear what he was saying spoken aloud. 'Perfect. You know, untarnished. This foul world we live in was going to destroy that. They had to be protected from that. Men were going to make them ugly and stupid and ordinary. Someone had to save them from all the brutish things that were going to happen.'

Angus said, 'But they were only children.'

'Haven't you ever wanted to have one perfect thing for
yourself? Something no one else could ever share?'

'But they weren't yours to take. You're not a child, you
must know you can't own people.'

Angus couldn't understand. He didn't want to understand.
To understand might be the start of forgiveness. He didn't
want to forgive.

Neil spoke in a whisper, almost as if he didn't want to
be heard:

'Don't you wish you'd never had to grow up?'

He was weeping now, though he seemed not to notice
the tears running down his cheeks. 'I couldn't bear it that
they'd grow up and turn into women like all the others,' he
said. 'I think I was too late for Tara, but the others . . .'

'You're insane,' Angus said. 'Don't you know what you've
done?'

'You mean what I've done to you?'

'No, not that,' Angus said. He was angry. 'What you did
to them?'

'I loved them, I didn't hurt them, I was so gentle, so
loving, and then I let them go to sleep so they died happy.'

His voice had changed; he sounded like a child talking,
not an adult.

'You're crazy,' Angus said.

'You don't have to worry, I've confessed to them all,'
Neil said. 'I've told them I'm the evil twin. I did that for
you. That proves I'm not the evil one, doesn't it? They'll
leave you alone now. You can't blame me for what's
happened to you.'

Angus laughed. It sounded so absurd he didn't know
what else to do.

Neil said in his new childish voice, 'All the time I thought
I'd got a sort of charmed life. The police arrested you and
it was like God was giving me permission to go on acting
the way I did. There was some higher power who approved,
you know? Can you understand?'

Angus said, 'I can't understand anything.'

Neil seemed not to hear him. He went on, 'And then
when Nellie told me about you, I couldn't take it in. It was

as though I'd got a chance not to be me any more. I could start again. The police were convinced you'd killed those girls. You were me, and you'd done what I did. It was like being reborn. But Joan was going to tell them, and Nellie too. I had to stop them.'

'You are insane, you know that.' Angus spoke as if this had suddenly, at last, become real to him.

'I suppose so,' Neil said, and he sounded bereft. 'But I don't feel mad. It all makes perfect sense to me.'

Sergeant Knowles pounded on the cell door and shouted, 'Time to go. Wrap it up.'

Angus got to his feet.

He said, 'Goodbye, Neil.'

He rapped on the door and Knowles opened it. Angus walked away down a corridor which smelled of bleach.

He cringed at the clang when the door of Neil's cell banged shut, and then the rattle of the key in the lock.

Angus thought it was the loneliest sound he had ever heard.

In the street outside, he took his mobile phone out of his pocket and called Sarah.

The drab grey street looked as though the sun had suddenly come out at the sound of her voice. For a moment, it took his breath away. And then he thought, my God, this is what it feels like to be happy.